LIFE HAPPENS...

A Novel

MARZUQ UMAR BASHIR

2020

Table of Contents

DEDICATION

To everyone out there who has loved and lost.

FOREWORD

SULEIMAN JAFAR & KHADIJA MUHAMMAD MAHMOUD

A written memoir on the bittersweet memories of the writer, narrating both sweet and ordeal experiences meted out on him. Although, the story is one-sided; it attempts to paint a rather agonizing pictures that are often left out for the newbies in the world of love.

This story further proves that our scars are a map of our unsavory experiences, that whoever survives them to home, emerges stronger and earns a medal of honor.

Our scars remind us that we are brave in a messed up world of fear and trepidation.

It is not the size of the trophy, but the thrill of the case.

In the end, all that matters is that life goes on. The good and bad memories, the pain, the heartaches and heartbreaks, the betrayals, all are governed by time for with time all will eventually slip into the dark shadows of the past although it's our choice whether to live in the past or not. Always keep dragging us to its domain like a magnet, and with time we will have no alternative but to let go of the past as long as we plan to live. And when we do, we will surly look back one day and smile or better yet, laugh at our experiences because we will always be what molds us into stronger versions of ourselves.

While it's true that I have gone through betrayals and heartaches, the optimistic part of me still believes that all that has happened, happened for the best things I have ever longed and wished for. After that, all these would prove to be worth it.

Pain, sorrow, happiness, smiles, laughter are parts of life, they all happen... and life happens.

CHAPTER ONE: A SPINNER AND A FAILED SPIN

It is true that we have both loved and lost, but it is also true that I have found and I love. Always, with her on my mind, I sleep, and with her, on my mind, I wake.

The first time I saw her, something about her got me. Her eyes, her eyes got me.

I caught her eyes and I looked away. I was tempted to look again, the enticement I couldn't resist. When I looked for the second time, it transpired again.

At that moment she ceased to be a part of my future, she quickly became a part of my immediate past. In that second; I was completely immersed in her present, just like she was in mine.

All I could wonder was who she was. For days all I could think about was her smile, how it gave me butterflies.

All I could picture was her ravishing face and her pretty eyes, how brightly they shone.

I just had to be friends with her, and with her I became friends. I had to spend time with her, and with her I spent time.

♪ *Some people talk about that love at first sight ish, to keep it real I don't know whether I believe it's true and if it is then tell me if I am wrong or right, if I fell in love with you before I ever even knew. I catch your eye and look away as if it never happened. Sometimes I feel as though I am caught up in a strange dream. If eyes could talk, then mines be telling you that I am feeling you, sometimes I swear your eyes be telling me the same thing* ♪

When she brought out and spun the spinner for the first time, it didn't spin. I noticed. The way she held its base with a touch so calm and tender, that too I noticed.

I had to hold hands with her, and with her I held hands. When I held her hand, I found a home. She woke up a feeling deep inside of me. So it all started with a spinner and a failed spin.

My feelings could perhaps be imagined, but could hardly be described. I fed on her love, drunk in love with her I was, still am. It was magnificent like being drunk, on water. Not Alcohol.

To be drunk on alcohol is offensive to moral sensibilities and injurious to reputation, to be drunk on Water is upright and euphoric. Drunk like that. Nevertheless, it was exquisitely painful.

The thought of not being with her the next semester hit me. One moment I was floating on love like a butterfly, and the other, filled with pain like I have been stung by a bee in its highest caliber of bad temper.

A certain emptiness made itself felt. A moment entwined with love and pain, both in equal measures.

♪ Club jumping, don't stop, off top. But you know we only go 'till 2 o'clock. Put your hood up, it's the weekend, drop that, back that ass up, and girls get to freaking. The last call at the bar, ladies get a drink, man get some courage. Ain't no telling you gonna see that girl tomorrow, Stop holding up the wall waiting for the right song. Better holla 'cause you know they bout to cut the lights on ♪

Being away from her made me realize how much I was in love with her. It's very hard to spend that much time with someone as brilliant and attractive and not fall for her. *Is it a mutual feeling? Why not tell her how I feel? I'll write her a poem.*

"Do you like poetry?" I asked.

She does, or as she said.

I had a plan, write her a beautiful poem, and hit her with that four-letter word. *What could go wrong?* It's either I get a *yes* or a *no*.

Not opening up means a certain NO. *Unless she feels the same and somehow decides to open up herself. How unlikely.*

I wrote the poem, but I didn't show it to her anyway. I felt it was too direct, too cocky. Really, what if she said no? That couldn't be a good thing. The feeling of rejection I couldn't possibly welcome.

It's very hard to keep such a thing to yourself, especially when you are deeply, madly, crazy in love.

I had to tell someone, and who best to tell than that person? So, I did, I let her know. Cryptic in a way, but she deciphered very quickly.

"It's complicated but I'll think about it" was her reply.

Hey look Amila, I don't care how complicated things get. I just want you.

"Take your time," I said to her, knowing deep down I didn't mean it.

See, I wanted an answer very quickly, a positive one. I was only glad that I didn't get a NO, yet. Then now all I needed to be was patient. After all, 'patience is a virtue' is what they say.

Before pouring out my heart to her, I asked her if she had a boyfriend. Believe me, I know what it's like to have someone you love dearly taken away from you, even though it hurts less when the person she is taken away by, is a stranger, but still.

"No" plainly, she answered. "If I have a boyfriend you would have seen him all over my social media".

Funnily enough, there was a picture of a guy up there on her twitter header. A while later, there they were all-over my timeline openly affirming their love for each other. *That has to be her boyfriend.*

Startled and perplexed, a sudden wave of fever hit me. My heart was shattered into small pieces, that couldn't easily be mended, like the pieces of a thin glass cup shattered on a hard floor finish.

Anyway, I did away with my thoughts. Somehow, I believed what she said to me earlier, because even as her friend I trusted her.

It's been a month, things were still as complicated and I still hadn't got a response. *Could she still be thinking? No way. Could things be getting more complicated now? That I don't know.*

I couldn't stop myself from thinking about her, always.

I needed someone to talk to, I needed to get things off my mind. What best way to cleanse your mind than to pour it all out?

I talked to a friend who was in school somewhere near the Nigerian border to a desert Country. I told him about a girl, and I told him about this girl. Faisal wanted to see her, so I sent him her picture.

My phone beeped, it was a phone call from Amila. Quickly, I answered and suddenly realized her voice was trembling as if she was in alarm of something, but she wasn't.

She was upset and her words marked out dissatisfaction. It turned out She was told by an acquaintance that he saw her picture in his friend's mobile phone and that his friend told him she was my Girlfriend.

My girlfriend. Wouldn't that be awesome? I didn't tell Faisal she was my Girlfriend. Perhaps he misunderstood. Of course, I wouldn't talk to him, I am not the type to judge.

I was sure he didn't mean to start mayhem.

"I am sorry that you are disappointed, I am sorry," I said.

"Yes, I talked to him about you but I didn't tell him you were my girlfriend" I added.

That was how the call ended. Although I have seen her wear a scowl on her face before, I have never seen her that distraught.

I followed her with a text message.

"For all it's worth, I wouldn't even talk to anyone about you if I don't have deep regards for you," I said in an attempt to soothe her away from her disappointment, but that seemed to not affect. Everything was to no avail.

Of course, she knew I have a deep regard for her, she knew. *But why would she even be this dismayed?*

Could it be that her friend knew the guy from my timeline, and she was afraid that he would tell him about her alleged disloyalty? That I didn't know. For some reason, I refused to ponder about it further.

Suddenly things between us changed. They were no longer as they used to be. They went from good to bad, fast replies to hours later replies, Baby to hi.

We still talked on the phone for a while though, only when I called or texted, sometimes I wouldn't even have my calls answered, most of the time. None of these calls were returned, but I kept on calling anyway.

Should I give her space? Perhaps, not too much space though, because I can't risk losing her.

So, I gave her space. Thinking she would notice my absence and hit me with a call or a text, or anything.

See, giving her space only added to my obsession. I thought of her all the time, I even dreamt of her a few times.

I remember before I left. Before things between us changed.

She asked me to promise her that I'll not forget her and that I'll come and see her. I promised.

Of course, I shouldn't be the only one making promises, so I asked her to promise me that she'll not forget me too and that she'll always stay in touch. She promised, and added, "Except I become very busy with school".

Fairly enough, but then I knew deep down that a promise shouldn't be subjected to any condition whatsoever. Unless it's not a promise, unless it's just a mere statement.

Maybe she is busy with school or maybe she is only trying to protect herself. After all, she once said I look like a player. I'd give her the benefit of doubt.

I could no longer give her space. I became tired of missing her, the unrequited love, songs that reminded me of her, love songs. I became tired of everything.

With all these suicide cases, Depression was the last thing I needed. I couldn't stop myself anyway, it's called love. I was in no way planning to break the promises I made. I am not the type to break promises.

Amila was averagely tall. Young and slim. She had a body almost the shape of a coke bottle. Her eyebrows dark and thin, and her eyes deep and wide like the ocean which was exquisitely outlined by her long and dark eyelashes just like the eyes of an Egyptian queen. She had a nose that wasn't too long nor short, thin and narrow, and a bit turned up in a ravishing way. When she moved her thin, but sexy in a way lips to speak, it was really hard not to listen for even the sound of her voice was soothing. Everything perfectly fitted in her slim V-shaped face. Her skin, tanned brown. She was my African Queen. She wasn't perfect, but she was perfect for me in every way.

Months passed. Her absence only made me grow fonder. Depression started to kick in. Every time I thought of her I listened to a 'The Weekend' song, which I, later on, realized it only sank me deeper into depression.

See I knew I had to do something about my doleful lifestyle, I was depressed. I had two options. It was either I let this girl go, or be more patient. I chose the latter.

It's easier to be patient than to let go of someone you love so dearly.

I went to see her as promised. She was still looking as beautiful, more dashing I must say. I fell in love with her all over again with fiercer urge and hunger. I forgot all that happened. *How I wish every day could be like this.*

We chatted for an hour which seemed like a minute. Seated on a park bench in the SUG (Students Union Government) garden of our school, we talked about music, school, friends, we talked about life.

I watched her sing the words to 'Mama' by Mayorkun, which now every time I listen to the song memories of her come running back to me.

"Let me have your phone," she said, and with a few clicks, she checked into my browser and downloaded the song into my phone.

It was a glorious evening that ended very quickly for me.

I never thought she would be that pleased to see me. That was not the picture I painted in my mind, and she did say she missed me. She even made me rename her on my phone, to something sweeter, something closer to the heart.

The way she looked at me almost made me believe she was in love with me. *What am I missing here?*

When I wasn't around, it almost seemed like she was trying to get rid of me.

Could there be some sort of a wall standing between us, a person, or a reason perhaps? I sure had no idea what was going on, but one thing was certain I needed to know for sure.

She woke up the feeling yet again, the feeling I needed so badly to be reflected by her.

Now that it seemed like she was in love with me, it was only logical to think that something was keeping us apart, I needed to know.

I was already aware of the guy from my timeline. *Could he be the one discreetly keeping us apart? I need answers.*

"Tell me about your ex and why you seem so insecure," I said to her.

"Because he was a Fuckboy (A boy who likes many girls and has short relationships with them)" bluntly, she answered. "End of Story".

But she was still in love with this chap, I've seen her post his picture once or twice. She was not over him.

The last time she posted his picture and added an emoji of a heart as the caption, I flipped. I decided I could no longer take it, the unrequited love, everything.

I told her to forget everything because her heart was somewhere else. She protested saying "My heart is nowhere", that she was just trying to focus on her semester examination, and that I was trying to use that against her – Moral blackmail

What she didn't know was how much I wanted for her to do well in her exams, better than anyone.

See I only wanted the best for her, but it was sad that she felt otherwise.

I wanted to give up on her and let go of everything, but I couldn't.

I will not call her again.

I ended up calling her again just for her to come up with an excuse and that she would call later, but she didn't call afterward. *Or maybe the word you should have used is 'never'. I'll call you 'never'.*

"You stopped calling me *baby*," I said to her in an attempt to pick her brain.

"No, not true," she said.

"When was the last time you called me anything sweet?" I added, knowing it had been long, very long that I couldn't even remember.

"Darling!" she said. *How funny.*

"And meant it, like you are in love with me," I said with courage, for I wanted to know for sure.

"I do, I am." She replied.

Wow! She's in love with me, isn't that beautiful? Finally.

Suddenly I felt like I was in a space with boundaries that seemed to continue forever, filled with roses, mostly red, colors reflected by a warm and blazing sun like I was in the garden of love. *If there is anything as such.*

I couldn't even think straight, all I could think of was spending the rest of my life with her.

I needed a confirmation though, 'I am' just didn't say much.

I wanted her to say 'I Love You', or even 'I am in love with you'.

"You are what now?" I asked again, thinking I would get a proper and straighter answer, but instead what I got was "I want to sleep".

No day passes by that I don't lose myself in the thoughts of her. Just like the sun to the moon, she lights me up inside. She is the last thing I think of before closing my eyes every night. I see her in my sleep, she is the girl of my dream. She is the first thing that comes to my mind every time I wake up in the morning, and just like the sun rises every morning, every morning I fall in love with her all over again. If she was a song, she would be my favorite song, the song I would always put on repeat. She is the last piece I need, she fits perfectly in my space. Until the sun rises from the West and sets in the East, until the earth is buried in the sun, until the end of time, I'll always long for her.

I was fed up. With the way things were going, I became tired and was already considering the option of letting her go. I made up my mind to just let go.

The truth is sometimes we just can't have it our way, most times we just can't have it all. I was ready to give up. *At least I should know how she feels. She should tell me 'No' first.*

"We have drifted apart," I said to her.

Her reply was "it's School".

She was starting exams soon but I couldn't possibly stand another long month of depression. I told her my mind, all of it.

I pointed out how she ignored my calls and whatnot. She said she was sorry, really sorry.

"At least tell me how you feel and I'll let you be," I said to her. I wanted to be done with everything, I wanted to make peace with myself.

"Okay," she replied.

"Yes?" I said to her in an attempt to force out a response.

"Yes," she said. *I don't get you. What do you mean by yes?*

"Yes, what?" I asked again.

"We can date," she said.

CHAPTER TWO: MISS SUNSHINE

In a moment of agony and despair, with all hopes of love gone and lost. In a moment when I wished upon a thousand stars to make my pain go away. In a moment when I wished someone would just hand me a gun and splatter the contents of my skull all over the wall, for the sad feeling of gloom characterized by a pessimistic sense of inadequacy was nearly unbearable.

Amid my darkest storm, when scary dark, and heavy clouds of pain formed in my skies. When the heavy winds conveying the feeling of worthlessness blew heavily in my soul. When I felt like a pariah. She came to me as a clear blue sky, bringing back sunshine to my life again.

She came to me disguised in an article of ravishing clothing, decorated with the tapestry of love, sewn stylishly with a thread of hope and happiness.

I believed her to be beautiful inside out. When I first caught her eyes, drool nearly came dripping out.

Thinking out loud, a treasure is what I have found.

She was like a peacock, admired by many others, that made me feel unique when she came up straight to me.

Suddenly, because of Miss Sunshine, I brought down my walls.

As soon as Miss Sunshine came into the picture, I quickly outgrew my old friends.

My old friends who stood by me when all hopes were lost and made sure all hopes stayed lost.

My old friends who kept me in the dark for a long time and away from the feeling of positive emotions of regard and affection.

My old friends who kept me from growing.

My old friends; Loneliness and Depression.

Brought down walls, and a constructed bridge. She lured me into her arms, and when I closed my eyes, she pushed me away.

There they were, my old Friends, running back to me.

Yet again, I fell in love with a disguise.

CHAPTER THREE: ASSAD AND MY LOST HOPE

Friday 14th December of 2017 started for me like a normal day.

Before getting out of bed, I composed and sent Friday greetings to some of my relatives like I normally did every Friday morning.

Shortly after some of the text messages have delivered, my phone started to ring. It was Uncle Mustapha who was one of the recipients of my greetings.

Uncle Mustapha lived in Sokoto state with his family. He was the type of man who was always generous and calls you just to say hi regardless of how young or old you are. *Indeed, big men don't make people feel small.*

"Hello! Bashir, how are you?" he asked.

"I am fine, good morning Baba" I answered very quickly.

"Abdul is coming to Abuja today to pick up Aliyu from school," he said to me in a very firm voice.

Suddenly I became very excited. Even before his phone call, I was already with the thought of traveling to Sokoto for the Christmas holiday before I move back home to Gombe to complete the rest of the holiday, and I have already planned my journey.

"Okay sir, I'll call him," I said.

I went to my place of industrial training like every normal day, except this was not just another normal day for I was going to travel the next day.

Work on site commenced by 8 am and closed at 17hours, even on Fridays. *At least that's what my supervisor told me.*

Where I worked was a remote location, at least 30km away from home. Yes, I worked in a construction site. Given my course of study, it was ideal.

Because of the remoteness of my workplace, to boycott the long and annoying Abuja traffic and reach my destination in time, at least a few minutes before 8 am, I would leave home just after dawn.

However, that very day everything was different. I was not even planning on going to work, but because I was going to give myself an early season's break (the site would be closed mid in the following week in anticipation of the season's break).

I needed to show my face and give out an excuse on why I was going on a break earlier than any other person in the company.

I left home late that morning, and to my surprise, the traffic was far from the norm. There was no hold-up. *Maybe I am so late for work that I have already missed the morning rush.*

I was already aware of what my excuse for coming in late would be. If I was asked.

I arrived at work a few minutes before 10 am wearing a traditional blue Kaftan and a pair of black loafers, and not safety boots, with no reflective vest or a safety helmet on. I was not dressed up to work.

I smartly sneaked passed my superiors' office that had its door closed, for I was not ready for any form of scold or interrogation.

On entering our office (an office room set aside for NYSC corps and IT students) I caught the eyes of that whom I was discreetly avoiding. What is he doing here?

"Welcome Sir" sarcastically, he greeted me. My heart skipped several beats.

As my face was flushed with guilt, my stomach grumbled to the tune of fear in my soul.

Busted! Ashamed by my failed stunt, I cracked up the corners of my mouth to force out a grin.

"Good morning" I greeted him.

His eyes returned to focus on the screen of his laptop computer, He didn't say anything after that.

I got myself settled in, and what followed was a midnight silence. He was working on his computer and it looked like he was in haste to move out of the site to attend to other business.

With my excuses already sorted out on the back of my mind, I was waiting and ready to be interrogated.

I was waiting for him to ask me why I was not dressed up for work or why I came in late to work.

About 30 minutes after, all he said to break the awkward silence glooming in the room was "you got stuck in traffic, yeah?" *are you kidding me? He is being sarcastic again.*

"Yes" keeping my cool, I replied to his question.

Despite coming in late, I was still planning on leaving early.

I came out of the office and stood by the door to look around the site and maybe get a thing or two on the progress of work so that I could report in my IT log book.

As I was looking for progress, Arch. Mukhtar rushed out of our office with his backpack gripped with one hand and his laptop computer with the other. He was rushing to move out of the office. *This is my chance, I need to talk to him now.*

I followed him outside the gates where he rushed to his car.

"I'll be traveling tomorrow, so I won't be at work next week," I said to him.

"You are traveling to Gombe, right?" he asked.

"No, to Sokoto" Sharply, I answered his question.

"Allah ya kiyaye hanya (safe trip)" he said and drove off through the rough and dusty road.

Since he is gone and probably won't be back until late in the evening, I think I should take my leave as well.

With Arch. Mukhtar out of the picture, there left no one around to stop me from leaving. I went back to the office, picked up my laptop bag, and left.

After visiting Ummi (a Mother), I returned home late in the evening where I lived with my Uncle, his wife, and his three kids.

Immediately, I informed Aunty Nafy of my plans to travel the next day and went straight to my room to pack my luggage.

My cousins arrived shortly after I have finished packing, we spent the night and left for Sokoto early morning the next day.

On the way, we passed through the city of Kaduna, and along Murtala square, we met several horsemen dressed in knights' Armor riding on the backs of their colorfully decorated horses and a very large number of men on foot with many amongst them dressed in oversized traditional Hausa warrior attire.

They were playing skillfully with shinning swords and iron spikes as they marched towards the gates of Murtala Square. *So, this is how our warriors looked back in the day.*

For a moment, I was not lost in the thoughts of Amila. The road trip was proving to be an escape from a feeling I hated.

With the Sun at its zenith shining brightly, music playing loudly, we sped off to Sokoto.

I spent the next few days in Sokoto and then returned To Gombe on Boxing Day. It was a break I needed, a break from the stress associated with working on a construction site, and most importantly a break from a depressing relationship.

Two days before my return to Gombe I received a phone call from an old friend of mine who was also my classmate when I was in High school.

Hamdala wanted me to play for our class team in a football competition which was meant to be part of the events in the upcoming Gombe High School old students' funfair and reunion.

He told me that the first Game of the competition was coming up on Boxing Day which also happened to be the day I would return home to Gombe.

I didn't have any football boots to play with. I wanted to get new ones in Sokoto but I didn't because I knew deep down I was not going to play. I didn't want to.

On my arrival home, I received a phone call from Assad. He went on about how I have been ignoring him, how the silence was too much. I dismissed his assertions and apologized.

He went on to ask if I was going to play in the next game of the football competition. I told him I didn't have my football boots but I'll check if I could get a shop that opens very early in the morning to purchase new ones, this was because our next game would kick off very early the next morning.

I was already thinking of changing my mind to just play because I thought there would not be a huge crowd to watch the game very early in the morning.

I slept very early that night and woke up very early to my phone's ring tone, it was Assad.

"Are you going to the Game?" he asked me.

"Yes, I think so" I answered with my voice cracked, a clear indication that I was just waking up from sleep.

"Stop by my place to pick me up on your way" he added.

"I left my Car in Abuja, but then Umar is coming to pick me up. I'll give him your number and ask him to stop by your place first" I said to him.

I didn't want to go all together, I was even planning on going out very early to my Grandparents' place, for the last time I was there was about two months ago in October when my Grandfather kissed the dust.

I called Umar and told him I was not going to the game, but he should please pick up Assad on his way.

Assad was an old friend of mine, one of my oldest. He was my best friend while I was growing up, the only person I trusted, and that whom I could tell anything to.

The first time I met Assad was in 2005 when I only came to Gombe for the holidays.

He came to our home with his Uncle to meet my Stepmom who was somehow related to them and she introduced us. Ever since then, we became close friends and he became the first friend I would make in Gombe.

Where he lived was not far from our abode, so we were often in the company of each other.

Most of his friends became my friends, and my best friend from Kaduna, later on, became his girlfriend. That's how close we were. Heck, we even looked alike. *At least that's what his mother (RIP) said.*

That morning when Assad and my other classmates played our morning football match I did not, but that same day was meant to be the final day of the competition, the day of the funfair, and also the final day of the reunion.

The day of the Funfair and Reunion was an opportunity to reconnect with a lot of people whom I have not seen in a long while. Since I failed to play in the football competition, there was no way I was going to miss the reunion.

I went to our grandparents' place with my cousin, Al-Musty. We planned on going to the Reunion together.

That same morning, I spoke with another old friend of mine Saeed who was planning on organizing his Funfair to promote his clothing brand.

Saeed, Al-Musty, and I arrived at the Gombe Township Stadium very early that evening where the Funfair and Reunion were going to take place.

The Funfair had not started yet. We stood by the football pitch conversing on how Saeed would make his Funfair work. He did have some pretty amazing ideas.

A while later and just as the final match of the competition was about to start, the Stadium was brimming with Gombe High School old students.

The game had started. Beautiful faces all-round the stadium watching. Grimaces, grins, laughter, old friends catching up on old times, football fans cheering, and the players doing whatever it took to win the game for their respective teams.

It was a beautiful moment to live in.

Meanwhile, I was seated in the mid-row just before the match kicked off when Suleiman Gidado came and sat next to me.

This person was very good to me back in the day when I was still in High School. We talked about old times, about the school, and our old school friends.

Suleiman was just asking me about my brains and beauty (as he referred to her) ex-girlfriend when suddenly my eyes turned its focus to a tall pretty girl that seemed to appear out of nowhere.

She was fair in complexion, exquisitely dressed in a black and white gown that fitted her so perfectly.

She was walking up with her friends in search of the best seat when I realized who she was.

It was Beeba, My Hope which made me lose all hopes.

Quickly, I looked the other way and acted as if I had not seen her.

A lot of people that I have not seen in a long time came up to say hi to me in the mid-row where I was seated with Al-Musty, Saeed, Magjee, and Sadiq Alkali who joined us shortly after the match had already begun.

It was a nice moment, well until Beeba showed up.

Love, the illusion of the weak. Is this really how it feels when you see someone from your past whom you have had dreams for, whom you were in love with? This is what I feel; the feeling of vulnerability, weakness, helplessness, hatred, and perhaps a little bit of love.

So, it's true what they say about love that when you truly love someone you never stop loving them, the only thing you could do is find someone you love as much as you did them or even more and get over them.

My mind raced back to the conversation I had with Abba Rio who was my course-mate and one of my closest friends, and Mahmoud.

Mahmoud was the first friend I made in the university, one of the geniuses in my circle who had at least a little knowledge about pretty much everything.

They saw right through me and said that if by chance Beeba ever came running back to me, I would welcome her with my arms widely opened.

Perhaps they were right, but then my pride would never allow that even if I was madly in love with her.

Suddenly, I became feeble. I was wanting in strength, both physical and mental. All I wanted to do was go home where I could be alone and sad all I wanted.

Somehow, I managed to look gay and exuberant when deep inside of me I was burned by the flames ignited by the treachery that came from that whom I had thoughts of a ring for, that whom I loved dearly.

It was mid into the game when we heard the call for Magrib prayer. I would go home and pray, but I was sure my friends weren't ready to leave just yet.

Magjee suggested that we go out to find a Mosque and pray.

Magjee and Sadiq Alkali have been friends of mine for a while. However, Sadiq Alkali has been my friend long before I met Magjee. I met him even before I enrolled at the university.

He was my roommate during my first and second year in school. He was the discreet politician and the unserious one who got good grades even without trying.

Magjee, on the other hand, was the real politician in my circle. I met him during my first year at university and we have been friends ever since.

We found a mosque just across the road from the stadium where the Funfair was taking place.

After praying, the three of us returned to the stadium.

As I set a foot into the gates, I farsighted Assad who was standing with Beeba, and a few of his friends whom I was acquainted with. *Just when I thought my day could not get any worse.*

I quickly brought out my mobile phone and began to browse through aimlessly. I knew they would see me passing by but I was still hoping they would not.

As we were passing, Sadiq Alkali stopped to say hi to our friends but I, on the other hand, continued to walk and did not stop as if I have never seen them before.

"Bashir!" Assad shouted out my name. *OMG! Is this guy trying to mess with me? Bros over hoes... yeah right!*

I turned around and went straight up to where they were standing.

Beeba stood there frozen like she was under arrest, well except her hands were not raised and she had her head bowed down.

I wanted to say something to her, anything. But then I thought maybe it was best if I don't say a word at all.

I said hi to the rest of the people in the group and left.

"Why did Beeba bowed down her head?" Sadiq Alkali asked.

"Shame, perhaps!" I answered and quickly changed the topic.

I was already down, talking about Beeba and Assad was only going to make things worse for me.

On my return home that late evening, I spoke with Khairiyyah who was a very good friend of mine whom I considered a sister and one of the very few people that happened to know about my love life.

She was also a friend to Beeba. I met her through Beeba.

I briefly told her about my day and meticulously about how I met the full of shame Beeba with Assad.

I wanted her to console me and tell me all was going to be alright, but instead, she began to tell me how my best friend was right to snatch away my girlfriend, how they were keenly in love, how life happens...

After a long conversation with Khairiyyah, I decided perhaps it was time I forgave them. I did, I forgave them but the infidelity was something I could never forget.

CHAPTER FOUR: LUCID DREAM

As I reminisced to the time when I was just a second-year student in the university, it came to me my lost dream, how I found love in a time when the word 'love' in my life was like a specie of an animal that was about to go extinct.

In a time when all hopes were lost, she became my hope and ensured my survival. My strength, she became.

She was like an oasis in my desert-dry heart which watered the love in me to its full growth. She was the cradle of every ounce of energy in me.

The prettiest thing I had ever seen and her shining eyes could make the sun go blind. She had a flair about her. Beeba was magic.

She was tall, almost as tall as I was. Her figure was so perfect, it made other girls look skinny.

She had a smile that could light up a whole town, her smile was electric. An assortment of brain and beauty with a great sense of humor. She was a masterpiece, perfection in its physical form. *How could one not fall for this Angel?*

In my head she was Beyoncé and I was Jay, and together we were drunk in love. My dream of her was seemingly real and vivid, it could cure blindness.

How I met Beeba was a divine will that went on to determine events that unfolded mysteries, mysteries I wished remain folded and stacked far away from sight like an unwanted mat.

It was very early in the morning of a Friday in 2015 when I received a downing text message from a high school friend of mine. Mashkur had lost his father, and he was inviting me to the funeral.

I called Abdulrahaman on the phone who was my friend and a classmate to ask if he was going to the funeral, he was.

He picked up Umaicy and me in his golden-colored Toyota Sienna from our residence and together we left for the funeral.

The three of us and our other classmates went together, and on our way back we stopped by to visit a friend.

Muslim was a straight-forward person and free-minded. Although he did things that the normal person would not even think of doing and one would even think of him irrational, Muslim is one of the most sensitive and balanced persons I have ever met.

We listened to music, chatted about silly stuff, laughed, and later on towards the end of the day snapped pictures.

I got a hold of Muslim's mobile phone and started to peruse through its gallery to see how fine we looked.

If the pictures weren't as fine as I wanted them to look, I was sure going to delete them. *Look at that. We look amazing.*

I surfed passed our pictures and found myself carefully scrutinizing a picture with several girls in it.

These girls were mostly pretty and dark in skin tone, but then there was this one girl that caught my eyes.

She was the fair tall girl with the exquisite figure who stood with her hand on her waist, her eyebrows slightly raised and mouth pouted.

She was truly ravishing. It was as if I knew her.

By closing my eyes, it appeared like I saw her ravishing in her simple dress, and there was a contrast between the straps on her well-designed flip flops and her indescribable feet that made her beauty more beautiful.

It is as if that was not enough, I had a feeling that her beauty lies in her simplicity.

"Who is this girl?" I asked, showing Muslim the picture.

Before he could answer my question, Pele who we were together with quickly answered.

That she was someone his best friend befriends. And that he once asked her to hook them up and she refused.

I vividly remember him saying I could not stand a chance with her.

I asked Muslim if he could hook me up with Beeba. It turned out Muslim didn't even know her, he only knew of her. So, I asked him to send the picture to my mobile phone through WhatsApp. He did.

That Friday I went back home very late in the evening.

All night I was disturbed with the thoughts of a beautiful stranger, I could not think about anything but Beeba. *I need to find this girl.*

I knew what her name was, the school she went to, and I had a picture she was in. with the little detail, I embarked on a quest to find my Cinderella.

A week had already passed by slowly. I had zero luck on finding this girl when it occurred to me, suddenly, to inquire about Beeba through Abdulmalik.

Abdulmalik was all about the latest trends and happened to know a lot of people in town.

I spoke with him on the phone.

"Do you know any Beeba from Gombe High school?" I inquired.

"Do you want her number?" he answered as if he read my mind.

"Yes please." Sharply, I answered.

He vowed to send Beeba's phone number the following day.

Later that evening I received an unexpectedly early text message from Abdulmalik, which I was expecting the next day. It was Beeba's phone number.

It was a moment full of excitement. The excitement I felt was so illusory, the kind of excitement you feel when you are being served your food after a long run of starvation.

Before getting her contact number, I thought to find her would be the hardest part of the endeavor. The joke was on me.

How do I even talk to her? Should I text, call her maybe? I hope she is on WhatsApp. Oh God! What should I do?

I decided I should talk to her on WhatsApp.

I saved her number on my mobile phone and went straight to my WhatsApp application and refreshed my contact list in the hope that her name would pop up. It didn't.

I was saddened by the fact that her name didn't show up. She wasn't on the app.

Her contact had been on my phone for a fortnight and I still didn't know what to do with it.

She was not on the only platform I could hit her up freely, and the sad truth was that the only way I could get to her was to ring her up on the phone which wasn't entirely a big deal. Well, except I had never done it before. Even so, I knew there is a first time for everything.

I knew this was the right time.

How do I start? What am I even supposed to tell her?

In my head, I planned and practiced all that I was going to say to her. My words, the words I would say to her were carefully selected and well-thought-out.

I picked up my phone and went straight to my contact list and scrolled down to her name. *It's now or never.*

As the rate of my heartbeat drastically increased, my hands started to tremble. I couldn't press the dial.

Suddenly, the air was getting lighter. The room I was alone in seemed to be getting smaller. I could feel the anxiety building up within me.

I quickly ran out of the room to get some fresh air, for I was being suffocated by the rapidly shrinking room and everything in it.

You coward! I took a deep breath to calm myself and went straight back to the room.

Finally, I dialed Beeba's number.

This time around I was confident, I had everything planned out. *What could go wrong?* After it rang for a second or two, she answered.

As soon as she answered, all my plans went into shambles. All the words I had an earlier sort out in my head were flushed away in a nick of time.

I told her who I was and where I got her number from, but not who I got it from.

The girl was proving to be stubborn.

I did tell her I was only interested in being friends with her, but all she was interested in was the person I got her number from.

I was not surprised when she asked who I got her number from, it was typical of these girls from my time.

I ran out of words. I couldn't wait to end the call, on an encouraging note though. I came up with an inane excuse, that I needed to do something right away and that I would call her again in a short while.

I dropped the call knowing I messed up this one chance. I was very sure she wouldn't pick up the phone when I call afterward, but I was an optimist.

In an attempt to recoup, I garnered more courage and after a few minutes I dialed her up again.

She didn't pick up. Of course, she wouldn't.

Okay, what should I do now?

I texted her right away.

She replied very quickly, and we went on chatting all night.

I don't know how I did it, but somehow, I managed to convince her to be my friend. It felt like everything was a dream, a dream I was wholly in control of.

Beeba and I became very close. We chatted through SMS (Short Message Service) all day and night, and never got worn-out.

She told me a lot about her personal life, her relationships, and whatnot.

We became each other's company.

What I liked most about her was how she carried herself. She was unpretentious and private.

In the era of social media, it's not often that you see a pretty dove like herself off all these social media networks.

What attracted me to her was her physical appearance, but what made me fall for her was her genius mind and beautiful personality.

With the way things were going between us, I knew I was going to fall for her. I fell for her.

I was head over hills in love and I truly believed she was the one. Now the issue was how to communicate my feelings to her.

I couldn't tell her, so I decided to show her.

It was noon, and I was already frustrated by missing her when she texted me. It was during her final days in high school. She went to school very early in the morning and returned late in the afternoon, and I was on holiday.

We were chatting that afternoon when she asked me how I felt about her.

I tried to change the topic, but she pushed on.

She knew I was really in love with her, but she wanted to hear me say it. *Don't blow this man!*

"I am in love with you" I answered.

I wasn't sure what she would make of that, or even what she would say next. All I knew is that the words said have been said, there was no taking them back.

Moving up and down, I was restless and impatiently waiting to receive her reply when my phone beeped. It was Beeba.

"I am in love with you too" she replied.

CHAPTER FIVE: THE SECOND CHANCE

I was awoken, dipped, and soaked in love. I fell in love with Beeba foolishly. I could do anything for her, I couldn't even die for myself but she was someone I could die for.

It was a funny paradox. For a person with no 'impossible' in his dictionary, to go a minute without thinking of her every day was an impossibility for me.

Falling in love with her was like magic, it happened with no explanation how.

We shared something unimaginable, the kind of love you only see in the movies. She became my Juliet and I was her Romeo.

"I love you," she said.

"I love you more" I responded promptly.

We kept on dragging who loved who more. Trying to be gentle and romantic, I knew I loved her more but I let it go.

"Forever?" I asked.

"Forever!" instantly, she replied.

Just like Augustus Waters and Hazel Grace who had 'Okay' in the movie *The Fault in Our Stars*, 'forever' became our thing. I was truly drunk in love.

My holiday ended, and I was off to school. Everything was going smoothly.

Assad was in school abroad.

When something so rare and amazing happens to you who do you tell? Your close friends...

I sent a picture of Beeba to Assad and told him about her, how I have found the one, the one I was going to marry. He was outwardly happy for me.

With my busy school calendar, I freed up time for her. I told her about all my daily activities and how every day went.

I lost my favorite uncle on a Friday evening, not long after I have resumed school. I was in the Mosque with Usman and a few of our friends listening to the preacher when I switched on my mobile phone.

Suddenly, notifications started to come in. The last notification that came in was that which got all my attention, A WhatsApp message from my cousin, Yasir.

Yasir was telling me about the demise of Uncle Jalo.

Before I could reply to his message, my eyes brimmed with tears. I showed the phone to Usman and didn't say a word afterward. All I could think of was sharing my grief with Beeba.

It's all about the first person you want to tell the news to.

I planned on traveling back home the next morning but Abba (my father) didn't see any need for that, so I stayed in school.

The day before I lost my Uncle, I called and texted Beeba several times but a response was something I didn't get. I was really worried about her.

The following day which was Friday, I composed a prayer and forwarded it to her. And shortly after the text had been delivered, she replied with 'Amen'.

I couldn't decipher what was going on.

I called her on the phone again, this time around some girl answered and told me Beeba could not get to the phone.

I was bewildered, I didn't know what to do. I decided to text her the next morning.

I texted her probing what was going on, and pointed out how I was really troubled. I wasn't even sure if she was going to reply to my text message or not.

"I don't think we should be together anymore" was what she said to me in her reply.

For goodness sake, I was already anguished and in a 'whatever' mood.

Like an injection, she induced the feeling of anger into my veins. I could feel it being mixed into my sadness and pain. The feeling formed within me was an unexplainable one.

Just like that, you ignored me for almost a week. And now this?

"Why?" I replied to her message.

She refused to give me any reason why she was breaking up with me, I wasn't even sure if she had one. All she wanted was a break-up. Things like that happen. Life happens, there is nothing one can do about it.

I didn't fight it. I went with the flow. Perhaps not fighting for her was the mistake I made, but what was I to do?

I had an awful week. I didn't only lose my favorite uncle, I lost the love of my life. My Juliet broke me and I swept myself away.

I was saddened all day by the words that came from Beeba. This was someone I loved dearly and that whom I could move mountains for.

The feeling of blue was nearly unbearable, it wasn't fair. She left me with no explanation and nothing but a broken heart.

Deep down I knew I haven't done anything wrong. I felt broken and I was down for some time.

Just like the sun rises every morning, I picked myself back up.

I wanted to completely erase her from my memory so I changed my phone number, I wanted to delete her contact from my phone, I couldn't.

Months passed, and I was living freely like a bird. For some time, I was happy and contented with my own company, well except the times when I listened to love songs.

I am the kind of person who doesn't speak much about his personal life, I find peace and confine myself in music.

Every love song reminded me of her, and I couldn't keep myself from listening to this kind of song. Perhaps that was what I wanted, to be reminded of her.

Her absence had created a humongous wound in my soul and these love songs that brought her close to me were like healing drugs to my wound. The drugs I constantly abused.

I was in a battle I didn't want to fight anymore. I missed her, and I knew it.

The Sacred Month of Ramadan was starting soon. Perhaps it was time I put aside my pride and ego, to lay down my sword.

I decided maybe I should call her and say hi. I was about to dial her number when I froze. I was nervous, filled with anxiety. Perhaps this isn't the best of ideas after all.

I gave myself a few words of encouragement. *If you feel something, you say it. If you want something, you take it.*

Instead of calling, I chose an easier approach. I texted her. I was cowardly brave.

I knew she didn't have my number, so I indicated my name in the text message I sent to her

She was seemingly happy with the text message she received. She replied quickly, telling me how my number had not been going through.

I knew why my number wasn't going through, but I kept it to myself.

It was mid into the month of Ramadan, and I was starting my second-semester exams.

This was my second Ramadan in school, away from the company of my family. But I wasn't uptight, all my attention was focused on the semester exams.

The exam wasn't entirely easy but we met the end of it in good faith.

In the coming session, we were going to be in our third year. But it's not as easy as it sounds. We have to go through the SWEP (Student Work Experience Program) first.

SWEP is an initiative by the university to increase its technical students in practical knowledge of what they are being thought in class.

It normally came up after second-year completion and just before the commencement of the third year. This meant instead of going home for summer vacation, we were expected to spend a significant part of the holiday in school doing practical works.

Even though we weren't going home, we were excited about SWEP. Even before the program, we have been talking about the whole thing, how we would play video games, football, and whatnot.

We have heard a lot about SWEP, how the classes start not too early in the morning and end very early in the afternoon every day, and how the sports directorate organizes football competition. The SWEP Cup.

We formed a football team with the rest of our friends. With Sadiq Alkali as our captain and Magjee our head coach, we registered for the competition.

In that competition, we were the team with the most fans. Maybe it was the name we chose for our team, and maybe it was our uniform jersey that gave us a little bit of swagger.

Barcelona was the name in every football fans' mouth. Surely, we were loved.

We got knocked out of the competition in the semi-final and played in the third-place against a team of our friends.

Our coach, many players including our goalkeeper failed to show up. As our captain, Sadiq Alkali went in as the goalkeeper and we picked Isah to assist as our coach.

The game was a beautiful disaster. We lost by five goals.

Sadiq Alkali who was our goalkeeper would come out in hope of scoring every time we got a corner kick and ended up conceding a goal every single time, he became famous amongst the fans.

Although we lost drastically, the game was the best in the competition for me.

For the entire program, I stayed in school in a hostel room Usman got for us. We stayed with Sadiq Alkali n and Khalifa.

I hated hostel life because of the congested rooms and partly because of their dirty toilets, but I was really glad I stayed in a hostel room during SWEP.

The room we stayed in clutches a lot of good memories. Every time I hear someone speaks of SWEP, our room is the first thing that comes to my mind, how we distressed our neighbors with our loud music from Sadiq Alkali's computer whose speaker sounded like that of the first generation 'Made in China' phones, how we drank khalifa's preposterously watery pap. It was quite an adventure.

Every morning we would wake up late, go to class, and return early. We did nothing but play video games and listen to music, and late in the evening, we would go to the newly constructed gazebos opposite the Engineering Complex for free internet. There weren't any plants growing around the place, which made me wonder why?

The place was being referred to as a garden.

When the internet speed was not as fast as we wanted it to be, we would go to the butterfly-like building which was just adjacent to the library staff car park that was opposite the school library where there was also free internet.

The internet wasn't exactly free, it was encrypted by passwords. Passwords were all names of the school lecturers. And luckily for us, we happened to know most of their names.

We used the free internet not that we needed it. All we did was download movies and listen to music.

It was a beautiful evening with exquisite weather. We were seated in our room with the cool and slow wind blowing our window curtains through the tiny holes of our window net.

'Work' by Rihanna was playing on the background when Isah came into our room and asked who would like to go with him to the Engineering Garden for free internet.

I was tired and exhausted by the football I played in the school field earlier that evening but decided there was nothing to do but sleep if I stayed in the space, and I wasn't ready to sleep that early. I picked up my computer and off we went.

About 30 minutes in the Engineering Garden with Isah, I was as exhausted by the adrift internet surf as I was by the evening exercise.

"How fast is the internet?" Usman asked as he came within reach of the gazebo where we were seated.

Even though the internet was fast that night, I had nothing important to do with it.

I decided to log into WhatsApp. I haven't been on WhatsApp all summer, for there was no one fascinating to chat with and the conversations were all mind-numbing if not disheartening.

I used to be on WhatsApp all round the clock but ever since I met Beeba it became a thing of the past, an old habit.

After the WhatsApp application had loaded, messages started to come in very large numbers which even made my computer froze for a minute.

I read and replied to some of the messages and left some unread. I went through my contact list and guess who I found, Beeba...

I was thrilled by what my eyes had seen. The sight of Beeba's name sent shivers down my spine, and my stomach grumbled with delight.

I was listening to music but at that instant, everything stopped in time, suddenly I became dumb and blind to all that was going on around me.

Quickly, I clicked on her name and started a conversation.

We went on to chat for hours that night. I have never been happier.

Even after SWEP, we unceasingly continued to have conversations on WhatsApp as friends even with the adoration we felt between us.

We were done with SWEP and with just a single week to resume school. Assad was back and was through with his 2-year study abroad.

With Beeba everything had changed, it was as if she was waiting for me to talk to her to resume our normal relationship.

With Beeba now on WhatsApp, In the process of making up for lost time, we became more affectionate with every passing day. Even though we were just friends, ours was far from the norm.

With just a few days to go back to school, I received a message that a guy I was acquainted with had just lost his father. Even though I wasn't that close to him, most of my friends were. I condoled him through SMS.

That same evening of Modi's loss, Aminu, one of my close friends, texted me on WhatsApp telling me he saw Beeba at Modi's residence.

He wasn't the only one amongst my friends that saw her that day, Assad did too. Just like myself, his breath was taken by her ravishing looks.

He had already started asking ludicrous questions about her when one of our friends told him who she was, my girlfriend.

I knew I needed to do something about my relationship with Beeba. The first thing I did was to ask her again the question she refused to answer. Why she left me with not a single explanation.

She didn't leave me because she didn't love me anymore, she left me because she loved herself more. She was still as in love as she was the day we became a couple.

Her alibi was that she kept on receiving text messages from an anonymous person, telling her how I would eventually leave her for someone better, how I would break her heart.

She got tired and decided to end it between us. And when I didn't fight it, she felt like her anonymous sweetheart was right all along.

But how was I to fight for someone who didn't want me?

I truly believed that in every relationship, communication is the key. My belief was the reason why I was utterly dismayed by the fact that she didn't tell me about the messages she was receiving when I knew she was supposed to.

Mistakes have already been made.

Now that everything had been brought to light, I needed to get back together with Juliet.

We were talking on WhatsApp when she started to talk about her friend and classmate who was almost as good-looking as she was and whom I knew from my childhood.

In an attempt to make her jealous, I began to ask ridiculous questions about Eman which I knew would subconsciously tell her I wanted her friend.

It worked, she became indignant.

Like a crying child that is being offered a candy bar, her obvious jealousy elated me to my bones.

As if that wasn't enough, I asked her to send Eman's contact number. And to my astonishment she did, she sent me the number.

I wasn't in any way interested in Eman though, all I wanted was the love of my life.

I deleted the contact, and after a while, she lightheartedly asked me if I called her friend.

I told her I didn't, and that's when she confessed that the number she sent was a made-up one. There was no way she was going to give me her friends' number.

"If I ask you to give me your friends' number, would you?" she thoughtfully asked me.

Like some retarded psycho, I replied to her with Assad's contact number extenuating my action with a thought that he was my friend and since I have already told him about her, the girl I would get hitched with, there was nothing to be anxious about.

She said she would call him and I dared her to, thinking she wouldn't. She went offline and came back on after a few minutes. She called him. I thought she was flippant about it all, I didn't have confidence in her words.

"What did you say to him?" I asked her.

"Bashir asked me to call you" she replied. I still didn't believe her.

Some minutes well ahead, Assad's call came to my phone. He asked me who the girl he had just spoken with was.

At that moment, I fathomed she wasn't flippant when she said she called him. I voiced out to him who she was, the girl I told him about when he was still in school.

After a few days of preparation, Al-Musty and I returned to Bauchi to pick up from where we left. Usually, at the beginning of the Semester before school gets tough we stayed in town in my Uncles' place where he lived alone then. This uncle of mine happened to be Al-Mustys' father.

The commencement of every semester was always my best time in school, this is the stretch when lectures haven't started yet and all there was to do was watch movies and play video games.

Muslim who had not yet processed his room in the school was coming to town the day after we have arrived.

I implored with him to come and stay with us and he agreed.

Even though there were two of us staying at home, it felt empty. We wouldn't mind another company.

The day after our arrival, Muslim came to town and arrived at our residence late at noon.

I was listening to music and conversing with Beeba on the phone when his call came in. "I am at the door," he said. Quickly, I stood up from the dark living room where I was seated.

 As soon as I pulled the front door open, the hot blazing sun hit me like an explosion in my face.

The brightness was too much for my eyes, I had to wait for a while with my hand on my forehead shielding my eyes from potential hurt by the rays of the sun.

Scrunching my eyes half-closed, I walked swiftly with my bare feet on the heated interlocked blocks trying to cut my way through the sunny opening and hoping not to hurt my eyes.

I found Muslim exhaustedly leaning by the outside unpainted wall of our gatehouse.

As soon as he came, the house lightened up a little, it was no longer as boring as it used to be when there were just Al-Musty and me.

We would wake up early, get ready, and leave for school. Getting to school we would all go our separate ways to attend to individual issues, but when its evening and time to leave we would all meet at a rendezvous point.

As we were all moving on with our normal lives, Beeba and I were relating well.

With every conversation, I had with her, my level of love for her increased. With every laughter we shared, I longed for her the more.

Deep inside of me, I could feel I was falling, tumbling head over heels in love with her again. I wouldn't mind getting her back. Even so, telling her I wanted her was something I thought I could never do again.

Every time I was not conversing with Beeba, I was either conversing with Muslim about her, or I was lost in the thoughts of her.

I talked about Muslim with her, she knew who he was. Considering both knew each other I decided to hook them up and as soon as I did, they hit it off in a nick of time.

He asked me what happened between us, and I told him everything. He knew she messed up, but he was still persuading me to get back with her.

Meanwhile, I was busy piling up feelings of jealousy within her, telling her all sorts of things about my female friends, how some girl was hitting on me.

I was playing with her mind, even went the extra mile to send her pictures.

I knew what I was doing to her, which was why I wasn't a bit surprised when she said she didn't like the girl.

Two nights before we moved back to school, I had a very long conversation with Beeba, it was as if she was fed up with all the stories I was telling her, all the touches of sarcasm.

She poured out all her emotions, telling me why she did what she did, and discreetly telling me she wanted me back. I didn't reply to all her messages and went straight to bed.

Fool me one time, shame on you. Fool me twice, there is no one to blame but myself. Is this really what I want? There is no doubt about that. There is nothing more beautiful than knowing if you fall, there will always be that one person around who is always ready to catch you. Is she that person to me? Everyone deserves a second chance, does she? Seemingly too good to be true. I wish there is a way into her mind, but do I want to find out what's going on in there? Heck, if she wants me, then I want her right back. Under my permission, my decisions to be clouded by my emotions. An illusion, the illusion of the weak that blinds the feeble. The presumed feeble, yet the strongest of all.

The morning greeted me with its warmth, all the energy I have lost in the previous day's activities was fully revamped.

I met a pile of messages waiting for my response, most of them came from Beeba. Before even replying to these messages, Muslim started preaching, hitting me with points after points on why I needed to get back with Beeba, and telling me how she was still in love with me.

Beeba didn't openly tell me she was in love with me, but she insinuated it.

I knew I was crazy about her, I felt it was only right to give it one more try. I asked her out again.

In a fraction of time, we emerged as lovers again.

CHAPTER SIX: THE ROLLER-COASTER

Form a mental picture of yourself riding a roller-coaster, a roller-coaster that only goes down...

The school was really frustrating, exhausting, and seemingly lifeless.

I found it very hard to concentrate every time I tried to study. I wondered in quest of a reason why. Maybe it was because I haven't been studying in a while.

SWEP turned out to be a fun time for us. And perhaps that's how it had always been with me and study every beginning of a semester.

Meanwhile, Beeba and I were keenly in love, the only time I enjoyed myself was when I was playing video games, or talking with Beeba.

I am the type of person who would choose video games over people, but with Beeba everything was different, just the thought of her made me lose concentration.

With just a few weeks into the Semester, another break was fast approaching. I was in great anticipation of Eid break, not because it was Eid, but because Beeba and I were planning to meet then.

Uncle Dahir, Al-musty, and I returned to Gombe the week before Eid.

Gombe is a 1 hour 30 minutes' drive from Bauchi, but it felt like an entire day's journey. *It is true what they say, you only hate the road when you are missing home.*

I wasn't sure if it's home that I missed or my Forever. Ever since I left for school we had been talking a lot about the Eid break, how we'd meet.

The journey wasn't very long, but it seemed like a journey of a thousand miles. I hated the road. I was filled with an empty feeling, there was a void inside me that I needed to be filled.

I remained silent with my cheek on my left shoulder, and my eyes fixed to the side window glass. I began to wonder how the trees seemed to be moving backward with great speed as we passed by them, even though I knew they were stationary.

Other than the crazy thoughts, all I could think of was home, and Beeba.

The moment we arrived my mood instantly bloomed like a rose flower. All the plants in our house seemed to be thicker and greener which brought me what I thought to be perpetual peace.

Dropping my luggage in my room, even before meeting the people of the house, the first thing I did was to call Beeba to relay to her how safe the journey was.

The following day a number of my friends came to me in the morning. We chatted for a very long while, and later in the evening when they were about to leave I offered to take them home.

On our way, Pele was just teasing me about Beeba when I farsighted a tall fair girl in a long white hijab, although I could not see her face clearly, I knew she was a pretty one.

"Speaking of the Devil, that's Beeba right there," I said to Pele, jokingly without the knowledge of who the girl was.

Suddenly, the car was as silent as a graveyard. Our eyes were all fixed on the three girls that stood far ahead. Well, mine was actually on the tall and fair one.

As we drove closer, her face became clearer. She did look like Beeba.

"Oh shoot! It is her" I said, with my heart beating quickly now.

I suddenly hit the brakes without even knowing it. Pulling myself together, I used both of my hands to brush my shirt and quickly got out of the car.

Beeba and her friends all set their eyes on me as they profusely smile.

I chanted the word 'Habibty' to her as I moved further closer. She was all smiles.

"How are you?" I said to her friends.

Without waiting for their response, I turned to Beeba.

"Habibty, how are you?"

"I am fine" wearing an even bigger smile.

"Where are you coming from?" I inquired.

Turned out she was visiting her friends.

It was very weird talking to her in person, I felt very uncomfortable trying to act cool. The conversation was very short. It was like the first time we met, which was even shorter.

However, we said our greetings and went our separate ways.

After dropping Abdul and Pele, all I could think about was texting Beeba. My thoughts were consumed by her ravishing self. If I had closed my eyes, she'd have been the only person I'd see.

We did make plans to meet up during the short holiday, but this was merely a coincidence. And it's in no way going to affect our plans.

******

The day of Eid usually comes with a lot of great feelings, every house is usually filled with family and friends.

However, I often find Eid Eve even more fascinating than the big day itself. It was a time when we spent most of the night watching TV, listening to music, and even playing video games, while the ladies in the house spent most of the night in the kitchen getting ready for the day to come.

This Eid was kind of empty, it didn't feel like it was Eid again, all the excitement, the anxiety that comes with the anticipation of the day we'd wear our new clothes and take pictures, and the Eid delicacies we'd eat. Everything felt off.

The event we used to be keenly in anticipation of every year didn't just feel like it again. Growing up makes beautiful things seem dull.

On the day of Eid, like always, we all got ready for mosque before 9 am. Al-Musty and I went outdoor to take pictures with Uncle Nur while we wait for Abba to get ready.

Most of the roads leading to the mosques were patrolled by security officers, some roads were even blocked. There were not too many cars on the streets, but the few ones were all moving to a mosque or coming back from one.

Jubilant faces all on the streets walking to the mosques majestically in their new traditional attires. The roundabouts were all decorated for the festive period, and billboards inscribed with Eid greetings mounted on the sides of the roads.

On arriving at the mosque, we found a place and laid down our mats. After sitting quietly for a while, we started hearing the sounds of a gunshot at timed intervals. It was part of the Emirates' undocumented tradition, shots to be fired every time as the Emir and his Entourage approached the mosque to lead the Eid prayer.

After praying, we drove down to our grandparent's place and gave our greetings.

On that day, I wore a brown kaftan with a hand-sewn dark brown design on the neck, a dark brown cap, and a pair of brown shoes. I wasn't sure if brown was my color, but I loved it, and I didn't care.

Faisal came to meet me at home just after we have returned from the mosque.

All I wanted for Eid was to see my Girl, and without an ounce of doubt in my mind I was sure she would look as ravishing and stylish as a peacock.

Later that evening, without even thinking about it, I picked up my phone and dialed Beeba's number.

I wanted to know where she was so I could go and meet her as agreed earlier. She gave me the address to her location, and we drove off immediately in the warm evening.

As Faisal and I drove near the location we were headed, I farsighted Beeba in a group of girls standing by the road as if they were about to leave for some other place.

On our arrival, I corrected the position of my cap and looked into the mirror to be sure of my appearance. Not that it mattered.

I got off the car to meet Beeba and her friends. There were four of them.

Beeba was beautifully dressed in a purple gown that formed a contrast with her complexion and brought out the glow in her eyes.

Our eyes locked and she smiled that electric smile. At that moment, there was nothing more appealing than the view of her ravishing face. My heart sunk, and I was lost in her eyes.

I said my greetings to her friends. She was still smiling, perhaps she was so overwhelmed with joy that she didn't even remember to introduce me to the group. I decided to save her the stress and do the introduction myself.

"I am Bashir" I declared, looking at one of Beeba's friends.

"We all know you," they all said in a chorus, with smiles in their faces.

I was in awe, my stomach was all butterflies. Beeba had told me that all her friends liked me, that she was evening starting to worry. I thought she was only pulling my leg. I was pleased and filled to brim with the feeling of joy. I felt Special.

Although, there was this one girl amongst the group that wore a black look all through our little conversation. But then it wasn't my business so I didn't give it much thought.

"Are you guys going somewhere?" I asked Beeba, considering where we met them.

"We are only going home" She responded in a soft voice.

"We are heading home too," I said. "We can drop you off."

Beeba was seemingly hesitant for a moment. She looked at her dejected friend, and her friend nodded in acceptance.

Faisal and I got into the car with the two of them, and off we went.

On our way, the two girls kept silent. Faisal and I kept on conversing, and he was teasing me about Chelsea (football club) when Beeba's friend interjected and declared she was a Chelsea fan.

"Finally!" I uttered. "Someone I am on the same page with"

"I didn't get your name," I said to her

"Khairiyyah" she answered. "I am Beeba's cousin that lives in a different state"

Beeba didn't utter a single word all through the journey. I wondered if she was only silent because of the topic of conversation, or because we were conversing with her cousin.

I parked just across the street from their house, and Beeba requested that we move a little farther away. As they got off the car, Beeba looked at me and smiled.

"It's nice seeing you," I said to her. "I'll talk to you later"

It wasn't my business, but I was a little relieved Khairiyyah wasn't as stiff as she was earlier.

"It's nice to meet you Khairiyyah" I said, and we drove off.

Later that night, I received a message on WhatsApp from an unknown number. It was a single 'hey'. For me, it was a normal phenomenon to receive a message from an unknown contact, it could be someone I was acquainted with, a family member or just basically anyone.

I replied as I'd do a known contact. It was Khairiyyah, she got my number from Beeba. *I thought you don't like me.*

I responded to her In the nicest way I could since this was my Girl's cousin, I even added a smiley emoji to portray my excitement thinking I would get the same energy in return. But funny enough, she stopped me in my tracks and made it clear that she didn't like me.

I didn't know if she meant it, or she was just teasing me. I was puzzled. *Why would she text me then, Just to tell me she didn't like me? That's absurd.* Anyway, I kept my cool and went on with the conversation.

"It looks like Beeba likes you," she said. "I have been trying to hook her up with one of my cousins, but she is just not cooperating"

"I love her very much," I said.

"I figured"

I was very much in love with Beeba, it was safe to say that I have never loved anyone the way I loved her. At some point, I wondered if I have ever loved anyone in my life before.

First love never dies, but my love for Beeba buried it alive.

"What I have with Beeba is pretty special, I have never felt anything like this with anyone before. I know it's going to be hard, and I know that there would be challenging obstacles, but I am sure we'll see past them together" I said to her, as honestly as I could.

"Obstacles like me" she declared, jokingly.

We joked about it, and somehow she was impressed. Even though I had no intention of impressing her, or getting her to like me, I was glad she did. In no time we became friends.

Some moments after, I texted Beeba to let her know that her cousin texted me, how nice of a person she was, and whatnot. I wasn't about any shady business, so I thought it was only right to tell her. I was very keen on keeping our relationship very open with zero secrecy. Well, at least on my part.

Beeba and I talked almost all the time, and with every conversation, I fell deeper in love with her. I was very enthusiastic about her, no matter how busy I got she was the one person I couldn't go a day without talking to. She had a great sense of humor, she found every lame joke I made comical. No matter how moody I got, just the thought of her brightens me up every time.

We talked about almost everything. I was fond of playing with her. I asked her about a song I listened to while I was growing up, and she didn't know the song.

"How would you know?" jokingly, I said. "After all, you were just a baby when the song came out"

There was a thing with Beeba and maturity, there was no way she was going to let it go.

We kept on dragging on the issue of the age thing. When it persevered, I began to ask her about old movies that I have watched to demonstrate my point. She didn't know any of them, except one.

"Oh! I know that one, Assad said I shouldn't watch it until I am old enough" she said.

"Assad?" surprised and confused, I asked.

"Yes, he talked to me on WhatsApp the other day"

I was further lost in confusion, I didn't know what to think or even make of it. So you have been talking with my friend all this while without my knowledge?

But it wasn't only about her though, I knew it deep inside of me. As one of my oldest and best friends, if he should ever be conversing with my girlfriend, at least I should know about it, at least he should have told me, and perhaps that was a mistake on his part, or not.

Slowly the feeling of regret started to eat deep inside my bones. There was nothing I could do, I couldn't even show her how hurt I was. This was someone I considered a best friend.

At the same time, I felt like nothing would ever go south, looking at our long history. And perhaps there was nothing wrong with my friend befriending my girlfriend.

On the day after the little conundrum, I went and visited Assad's Mother. She was a person I think very highly of, she was like a mother to me.

She was a humorous and generous person. I visited her every little chance I got, even when Assad was in school. When He told me she was sick I didn't think it was very serious, but when he vaguely disclosed the details of the sickness with me I felt weak and nearly burst into a pool of tears.

However, on the same Eid. My cousin Al-Musty went with a couple of his friends to Beeba's place of residence, for they once had a history with the family. He was telling about something that transpired there when his tongue slipped and he told me he met Assad with one of his friends Muazu who shared the same history with the family.

I found myself rolling deeply in perplexity. This was someone that didn't want me to park in front of their house. On top of that, neither the two of them related to me about the visit. *This is the red flag, from now on, I observe.*

I wasn't about to make any speculation. I felt I wasn't supposed to judge, but deep inside of me I knew something was wrong.

Later in the evening when I spoke to Beeba. I asked her how her day went, and who visited her that day, and if she had fun. I knew it that moment that I didn't really care how her day went or who she had to host, all I wanted is for her to tell me about Assad's visit.

She told me Muazu visited, and they had fun conversing. I waited for her to mention Assad's name, but I wasn't surprised when she didn't. I had to quit being discrete and ask her straight up before she told me.

I was at the school library with Yaro who was my study buddy on a Monday morning not long after I have returned to school when my phone started to ring, it was a call from a friend of mine who was then in his final year.

"Where are you?" a girl asked, in a soft and soothing voice. "We are in your school"

"What?" I asked in a perplexed voice.

Before the voice could utter another word I had already deciphered who it was, Beeba.

I could hear Sambo's Voice from the background asking her to pass him the phone.

"Come to ATIL by the school gate," Sambo said hurriedly and dropped the call.

At that instant, I told Yaro I would be back in a jiffy and took the road to the school gate.

ATIL was a fancy eatery that was established not very long. The view of it always amazed me, but ever since its opening I had never been there before.

ATIL was surrounded by a short perimeter wall in the colors of the main building and designed at the top with metal casings. From the outside of the gate, one could see a gazebo perfectly positioned in the compound which added to its esthetics.

The main entrance door was made of tinted glass, outlined at the edges by red-colored aluminum planks which accurately brought out beautifully the colors of the building.

I was a little nervous to meet Beeba that abruptly. I knew she was in town but I didn't know she would be coming to our school.

I went into the restaurant and met Sambo, and Beeba who was in the company of her friend, and the three of them were seated on one of the dark grey glass tables by the right, they were waiting for their orders. But I was fasting then, I felt like it wouldn't be a pleasant view seeing them eat.

I dragged out the chair that was directly opposite to Beeba. Immediately after taking my seat, I brought out my phone to take pictures of Beeba. Forgetting my flash was on, it flashed and the poorly lightened room lightened up for a few intervals.

If there was a way I could bury myself, I would have. However, I swallowed my embarrassment and started again. She covered her face all that time, but that didn't stop me.

After I have managed to take a few more photos of her, she asked for my phone and to my surprise, she deleted the pictures. It was awkward and very embarrassing. I didn't know what to feel.

I got my phone back and snapped another picture, she covered her face again. *I don't care, you can put your head under the table but I'd still take pictures of you.*

Part of her right arm which she used to block her face was covered by her black veil and the part that wasn't showed her skin whose color complimented the orange circles on her dress that made the picture even more beautiful than the ones she deleted earlier.

Some moments after we have parted ways, I found that one picture that survived her purge and used it as my WhatsApp profile picture for a while.

A few nights after, Khairiyyah texted me, she was really sad and hurt by what transpired between Beeba and herself.

While I was all lovey-dovey with Beeba, our friendship with Khairiyyah grew stronger. I seek advice from her whenever I needed one, and so it was the other way round. She became more like my sister, and I was her brother.

To complete our circle, Khairiyya thought because since she was related to Beeba and now like a sister to me, there was nothing wrong with being friends with Assad who was in both of our lives.

She sent him a direct message on Instagram, where they engaged in a little conversation. She introduced herself to him as Beeba's cousin.

Shortly after, Assad took screenshots of their conversation and sent them to Beeba. She took it the wrong way and started to question Khairiyyah.

On my part, everything felt off. I mean, I didn't get why she would be mad because a person she is related to talked to a guy that she befriends. *Are they friends, or what's her plan?*

I couldn't begin to fathom what was going on right under my nose.

Subsequently, Beeba posted a picture on her Instagram page. I liked the picture and made a comment under it that discreetly showed we were in a romantic relationship.

Some moments after, I noticed the comment I made got deleted. I spoke to her about it, and she came up with a crummy justification that her sister goes through her comment sections often. *But how was that a problem?* Anyways, I let it go.

I refused to comment on any of her subsequent posts. However, I noticed Assad commenting on the posts in a romantic tenor and I found it funny that she was reacting with the same energy. *Where is your sister now? I smell a dirty rat.*

I didn't raise any alarm. I believed that what is true would always come to light no matter how hard we try to cover up. In the end, the truth always triumphs.

Another picture was posted, and another comment was made. However, this last one and the reply it got cleared my doubts. I wasn't only smelling a rat, the beast was right in front of me and I could see it evidently with my naked eyes.

Beeba expended some of her childhood days in the Middle East, there she learned the Arabic language. The few Arabic words that I knew, I learned from her.

When she posted the picture, all of my interest was on the comments made. Assad said something really sweet to her with added an emoji that was nothing short of affection.

"My Albajnam" she replied his comment.

It sounded like Arabic. And considering her background, it just got to be. *I can't know for sure until I ask.*

For me, that was the last straw. I was sure something was up, my intuition could not lie to me.

"Albajnam," I said. "What does it mean?"

I was dead serious interrogating her. The conversation became heated.

She said she didn't know what the meaning was. But she explained that she was texting him one night and she was very sleepy, She typed in a random word and sent it unknowingly. In the morning after she had woken up from sleep, and Assad asked her what it meant.

"My favorite," she said.

That was it. As her boyfriend, I knew I should be her favorite person, not anyone, and not my friend.

"Your favorite?" I cautioned.

"Yes," she answered plainly.

"My favorite person," she said.

I can't say I didn't see it coming, because I did.

"If something is going on between you two, I think now is the perfect time to say it," I said.

She knew where I was heading, it was obvious. She asked me if I was okay, really okay with her being friends with him, cause she couldn't fathom where I was going with the conversation.

If I am right about you two (which I know I am), and I tell you I don't want you talking with my friend, I know you'd run to tell him.

I decided to end the conversation right there before it got out of hand. The truth always triumphs.

Assad's mother was seriously ill, she got admitted to the hospital. I was still in school and I couldn't go to see her.

When I told my elder sister Fatima about her ailment, she decided to pay her a visit at the hospital.

On her visit, there, she met Beeba with Assad. Of course, my sister told me she met my girlfriend.

In an ideal sense, there shouldn't be any big deal in that. But there was everything wrong with it. She didn't tell me she was going to visit my friend's mother, I had to find out from my sister.

After my sister had told me already, Assad sent me a picture he snapped Beeba and added the caption "guess who came to visit"

He told her the pictures he was taking her were for me.

Not a word from Beeba. I was going through my social media then I saw an update she made. It was a picture with a text inscribed on it. It was about finding the perfect guy, who is romantic enough to take pictures of you spontaneously.

"And when he does, make sure you don't delete them," I said to her.

I knew she was referring to Assad, but I was still trying to push out the truth from where it was buried.

Beeba applied for a University in a different state, and they were called for Screening. The same University Khairiyyah was a student.

She traveled for that purpose, and Khairiyyah and her parents hosted her in their home.

The day after she traveled, Khairiyyah texted me.

"Beeba is a very good pretender," she said.

Of course, she is. I knew it, and I have a feeling I know what she's been hiding.

Khairiyyah refused to disclose what was going on. I tried to pick her brain but all to no avail.

She asked me to send her Assad's' contact. I remembered what transpired between her and Beeba when she sent him a message the last time.

"What are you up to?" I asked.

"Don't worry bro" she replied. "I won't do anything you won't approve of"

I could feel it deep inside my bones that something bad was about to happen. I sent her his contact anyway.

The part of the state where my friends and I rented an apartment wasn't very far from our school. However, there wasn't enough supply of electricity. We went to the school where there was stable electricity to charge our gadgets every day.

That Saturday morning before I left for school, I was talking with Mahmoud when my phone started to ring. It was Assad.

I answered the call in a jovial manner that I was used to, but Assad wasn't really up for it. His voice was firm and strong, with all seriousness.

"Who is this Khairiyyah?" He asked.

"Oh, she is Beeba cousin" I answered. "Is there anything wrong?"

"She texted me on WhatsApp, telling me all sort of things. That I know I am your friend, and I should watch my relationship with Beeba before anyone gets hurt" he said in a shaky voice.

"Wow! She did?" I asked

"I don't want these girls to come between us. I can choose to stop talking to Beeba. My relationship with you is more important to me" he said.

Considering what happened the last time, I knew if Beeba came to find out, a very ill-feeling between her and her cousin would come about.

There is no way I'd be the reason for a falling relationship between two cousins who have been friends since childhood.

"You know how girls can be. I'll talk to her, just don't say a word to Beeba." In an attempt to curtail a wildfire, I said to him.

"So I shouldn't talk to her?" he asked.

"No, you shouldn't" I confirmed.

"The only thing I know is that there was this one time I was talking with Beeba, then I asked her about you like I normally do. She told me she doesn't love you anymore Bashir" he added.

But why are you just telling me now? If you are truly my friend, you would have told me this earlier.

I was hurt. I didn't know what to think. I was riding on a dead horse, I knew it was just a matter of time. But I was hurt.

"She said that?" I asked.

"I asked her to tell you by herself, and I don't want to talk about it," he said.

"I'll talk to her," I said. And the call ended.

I was in shock. I knew in times like this, our emotions tend to overshadow our judgment. I was hurt, and heartbroken. It seemed like everything was just a dream.

In my mind, I had already calmed Assad's nerves. I was sure he wouldn't do anything absurd.

Before I could talk to Khairiyyah, my phone went off. I went straight to a friends' room in the school to get my phone Charged.

After getting my phone plugged, a couple of my friends and I went straight to the library to study.

I was stuck on the first page of my book. I couldn't study a bit, I spent hours without actually reading a thing. My mind was full of thoughts, trying to solve puzzles I already knew the answers to. Despite everything, I was still in denial.

I closed my notebook and went straight to the school hostel to get my phone.

I got my phone. I was walking back to the library, deeply lost in my thoughts. I looked up and saw the reflected sun rays that formed blissful beams of light by the clouds partially blocking the sun. It's nothing short of beauty, for a moment, I could feel my worries fade.

I got into the library and sat next to Yaro. My phone was already kicking.

I sat quietly as it loaded, I was lost in my thoughts again. The phone in my palm started to vibrate, and I was snapped out of my wonderland. Messages from different contacts were coming in rapidly.

A text message notification popped up with a preview that reads "hey, please call me. It's urgent."

I was really worried, I went out of the library and sat by the parking lot. I tried Khairiyyah's number, there was no answer the first time.

I tried to call her again and this time around Beeba answered. At that moment I knew she had already found out what I didn't want her to.

"Where is Khairiyyah?" I asked the way I'd ask a stranger.

"She is not around" she answered in the same manner.

"Tell her to call me back" I dropped the call and went back inside the library.

I could feel everything crumbling and falling apart like a city amid an earthquake disaster. There was nothing I could do to stop it.

After spending long hours in the library without studying, it was dark already and time to pray Magrib prayer.

We went out and walked down to the mosque. On our way, I received a message from Beeba.

"Hi," she said.

"Hey. How are you?" I replied as if nothing ever happened.

"I am mad at Khairiyyah," she said.

"Why are you mad at her?" I asked, in an attempt to make her speak up.

"I am mad at the both of you," she said, bluntly.

I knew she had found out. The question I couldn't figure the answer to was how she found out. I specifically asked Assad not to tell her and let me talk to Khairiyyah.

"Because I called her?" I asked

"No. I am so mad and disappointed that you think I'd do such a thing." She said.

She asked me if I knew what khairiyyah had done. I told her I did.

Beeba was trying to pin it all on Khairiyyah and me. In defense of Assad, She blamed us for everything. And not herself.

She didn't care to explain the accusations on her, which I felt she was supposed to if she cared about my relationship with her. But that was the truth surfacing.

She was so keen on protecting him, that she didn't even care what I thought about the two of them.

"Hey! Why are you trying to pin this all on Khairiyyah and myself? I don't know what it is between you and Assad, all I know is that Khairiyyah was only looking out for us because she cares about us and our relationship, and for that, I'm even grateful." I said, to cut her tantrum short.

I didn't expect everything between us to go back to how they were from the beginning, but I hoped.

Our relationship was fading faster than I anticipated. I couldn't believe I was going through this same road again. No one ever told me that love was supposed to hurt.

I needed someone to talk to, but even Khairiyyah wasn't there anymore. After what happened, she promised herself never to interfere in our relationship again. As I expected, the bad blood between the cousins grew thicker.

The days that followed were the days of torment. I went to the library every free time I got not because I wanted to study, but because I wanted to have my mind freed.

I laid down my head very early at night to sleep but often ended up thinking all through the night alone in the dark. The night became my friend. The time I was happy, I was filled to brim with sadness. Thoughts were cacophonies in my head that nearly drove me crazy.

Mahmoud was the only person that noticed my silence and deciphered my expressions. He often asked if I was fine. In my answers, I was always super.

Every time I texted her, what I got was a one-word reply. I wondered if she was like that with Assad after what had transpired. We never spoke on the phone, we barely even texted.

Even when things were in shambles, I still loved her.

It was all bad, very bad. I was getting used to being depressed and living without her love that I wish I had never tasted. *If this is what love is, then I don't want to love anymore.*

We had a very long conversation on WhatsApp as if everything was all good between us. Even though I was sure something was going on between Assad and her, we never broke up. I was still holding on to the girl I love.

Our conversation was about to end. She was short on battery life.

"I love you" sincerely, I uttered.

"Me too"

I was the type of person who is very sensitive to the issue of love, there was no way I would let it go. This was someone that always initiates an 'I love you', and when she didn't, her response to it was always 'I love you more'.

"Hey, if you don't love me anymore just tell me. We should stop wasting our time" bluntly, I said.

"It's not that I don't love you anymore. I still do. But I am in love with my ex, and I am always spoiling your mood" she said.

"I need time" she added.

Seeing these messages, I knew what was going on. She was trying to use her ex to get out of our relationship.

I shook my head and kept my phone aside. I could hear the click sound my mobile phone made every time there was an incoming text message.

Her messages piled up in my phone. All of the messages were an explanation, or justification for the maltreatment channeled towards me. None of these texts messages talked about a break-up, none of these messages deserved my response.

She called my phone about 15 times, I didn't answer any. I couldn't bear listening to her voice. I felt betrayed.

My stepsister called me and was asked me what was happening between Beeba and myself. I didn't disclose anything.

"Beeba told me you two broke up, tell me that's not true."

"Well she told me she is still in love with her ex, but we didn't break up per se," I responded.

It turned out that my step sister asked her to make things right, and she snubbed. That we should leave her alone, if I could wait for her then that's fine.

Since that was the case, since it has reached that, I decided to bury the dead horse. The love affair was a roller coaster, and it was time for me to get off the ride.

I went back to her pile of messages.

"It's okay. I understand." I replied. And that was it.

CHAPTER SEVEN: LOVERS-BAY

On the long road to Lovers-bay, I missed my way. I found myself on the road to destruction. My navigator betrayed me and I drowned in confusion.

I was lost and I had no intention of finding my way back.

I began to ponder over how soft I have become over the journey I wish I had not embarked on.

If this is what love does to one, then blame me not when I say I don't want to love anymore.

Everything has its cost. With the cost this high, I wonder, was it ever worth it?

I gave my all and what I got back was a dilapidated self-esteem, self-worthlessness. I had no option but to miss the old high-school giddiness, it was lit.

I didn't sign up for this, I missed the old me. I missed the young boy with bright laughter, the boy with the flamboyant attitude that was admired and loved by many but never loved in return. The heartbreaker, and never the heartbroken.

What goes around, comes around. The words that kept running in my mind.

Could this be karma catching up to me? I wondered in awe.

I know I have broken a few hearts on my way here, but I have never betrayed anyone like this I swear.

I saw it coming, I did see it coming.

It was like being told you are going to get punched in the stomach. You can see the Fist locked and knuckles tightened, you see the arm swinging the Fist towards you. But as soon as the punch drops, it still hurts you.

I am going back to where I came from. The road to Lovers-bay is crooked and full of darkness.

Maybe it's not meant to be my home. To myself, I say this in all fairness.

CHAPTER EIGHT: THE AFTERMATH

In this life, the only person that can hurt you is the one that you care about. I was hurt.

When she said we would forever be together, I thought that meant at least for the rest of our lives. I guess the joke was on me, forever wasn't as long as I thought it to be.

For a moment, my heart was a lonely winter subdued by all the negative emotions that blew through my soul like a soft wind through the leaves of a tree as it made a rustling sound to my deteriorating self-esteem.

The aftermath came with a near-complete lack of contact with the outside world, long sleepless nights accompanied by over thoughts, and loss of interest in usually pleasurable activities. My mental health was hanging in the balance.

For weeks I puzzled through the awful memory in my head, nothing made sense, I knew the pieces would not fit. I tried very hard to make meaning out of what I knew had no meaning. It was like running in a hamster wheel, I was in motion yet I was stationary.

My behaviors changed without even realizing it. What I went through made me develop trust issues. I no longer mingled with people around me, I confined myself in my thoughts.

I was leading a miserable life. The over thoughts became unbearable. Often, I went to bed as early as 8 pm and got up as early as 5 in the morning.

I knew it was bad when waking up in the morning all I looked forward to was going back to bed at night, and the sad reality was I couldn't tell anyone because I was too afraid of being judged.

Yusuf was the only person I could talk to amongst my best friends without the fear of being mocked or judged, and he was far from reach.

People often see depression as weakness or unmanly, but in reality, it has sent a lot of innocent souls to their graves. *I wish the world isn't as messed up.*

Perhaps I loved her just a little too much, perhaps I wasn't good enough for her, and perhaps it was the betrayal. There were too many reasons to ponder on and enough blame to go round, but the only person I blamed was myself.

My social life was wrecked. My social media networks were all boring and depressing as if I needed more depression.

The days passed, the memories would last forever. I woke up in the morning and the day joined to mourn my emotions. The sun was blazingly hot, leaves on the trees were on a standstill, and there were no singing birds or bleating sheep. My heart stiffened. For a moment, I was filled with rage rather than disappointments.

I went on Twitter. Bitter the words, I poured out my heart. Sambo noticed the series of posts I made and the tone they were drafted in.

"Do you want to talk about it?" he asked.

I was hesitant for a moment. This was Beeba's cousin, I was afraid no matter what I told him, instead of listening he would Judge, and offer his judgment in prejudice. But to my surprise, he was nice and supportive.

When I poured out my mind and told him how I felt betrayed, I didn't mention names. He spoke as if he knew she left me for my friend, which was contrary to the reason she gave me when she was leaving.

He advised me on the whole issue and told me that I needed to talk to them, get closure, and stop blaming myself for everything.

But there was no way I could talk to them. I'd rather just walk away and move on. But that was the tricky part, moving on.

Assad had been texting me. That he wanted to speak to me about something. I parted ways with my girlfriend who was his friend during our relationship, I thought he knew, but I wasn't surprised when he didn't talk to me about it. I told him about the break-up. Apparently, he heard about it.

Sometime after, I was leaning on a pillar by my desk in the library studying for a test I was about to write when his call came in.

Speaking on the phone was against the rules of the library and one could get his device seized if caught. However, I wanted to hear what he has to say. I answered.

"Hey, how are you?" he asked in a confident voice.

"I am fine" I whispered.

"How is school?" he asked, sensing I was somewhere I wasn't supposed to be on the phone. "Are you busy right now?"

"I am at the library, but we can talk," I said.

"I have been wanting to talk to you about something. It's Beeba," he said.

"What about her?" I asked. I was suddenly in deep inquisitiveness.

"She said she likes me, and I am feeling some type of way about it. And I am in shame" he said.

Oh finally, someone decided to tell me the truth. But I was already in the knowledge of what he was trying to tell me. It didn't matter anymore, the damage has already been done.

"Oh, it's okay. It's not like we are together," I said

That was how the conversation ended.

I told Muslim all that transpired. It seemed like he was overwhelmed, and was somehow in doubt.

Another Eid break was coming up soon, and the exam session was soon approaching. I was in school, and I didn't want to go home. I didn't want to meet any of them.

I decided not to go home, and I used the upcoming school examination as my alibi for not returning. That was my very first Eid away from the warmth of my family. It was a sad and beautiful experience.

Eid in Bauchi was nice, it was what I needed. Al-Musty and I spent most of the period with Usman, Sadiq Alkali, and other friends that I made during my stay in Bauchi.

We went to watch the Durbar. It was ravishing, the display of ancient culture. It was amazing how many people were willing to stay under the burning sun just to watch these displays.

It was still during the rainy season. We stood just across the street in the grass that was still wet from the previous days' rainfall.

The rich green leaves on the trees were slow dancing to the tune of the soft cool breeze blowing in intervals letting down the little rainwater they held as the brightness of the sun complimented the ravishing colors of nature. The smell of the grass as they were being matched on released the dopamine in me and I was excited for no reason.

I was living in the moment. And in that very moment, nothing else mattered. Staying in Bauchi proved to be a great decision.

There were so many people, and many whom I was acquainted with in school that couldn't travel for the break were there. Because we came late, we couldn't get to the front. We decided to capture the beautiful moments in Photographs.

After the Durbar, we went back to Usman's place and from there we left for home.

I was just about to go to bed very early that night as I was used to when Muslim texted me.

There was a barbecue gathering that held in Gombe, many of our friends went. Assad went with Beeba as his date.

I knew that would happen. Perhaps it was one of the reasons I stayed back. I couldn't even imagine how I'd feel if I was there. More than ever, I was very glad I didn't go home.

Before everything, I kept a lot of friends. Everyone was my friend, my mom was even complaining. I finally realized how true the saying "it's not the number of friends you keep that matters, it's their quality" is.

It has been a while, I was still in pain. Almost everyone that was involved has forgotten. But there was no way I could. Well until I heard the news of Arya's death.

Arya used to be someone Yusuf was truly in love with. We used to talk a lot about her. Though they never got together, for me, she was the best amongst all the girls he has ever been involved with.

She was young and by far the prettiest girl I had ever seen, and by what I heard, her heart was as ravishing as her face.

I was going through my social media then I bumped into a picture of her with a grieving message as its caption, posted by one of my secondary school friends. Cancer got the best of her.

I couldn't believe what my eyes had seen, I was feeble and emotional. Yusuf was the only person that came to my mind, I knew how much he loved her. My mind raced back in memory when we had conversations about her. How he was very excited to talk about her.

I spoke with him on the phone. Even though he was trying to be strong, the cracking in his voice let him down. He spoke with energy that couldn't match his usual self. He was anguished by her death. He was heartbroken.

Everything she had been through, all the words she had spoken, all the places she had visited, and all the places she had planned to visit didn't matter anymore. She was gone, gone for good as if she never existed and there was nothing anyone could do. She was nothing more than a memory.

At that moment I realized that whatever it was that I have been through was nothing more than a memory.

In the end, everybody dies. Life happens, and when it does, it does. We can't explain it even when try, the only thing certain about it is death and we are all going to die someday. Everyone you meet is just a fading memory, and some memories fade faster than others.

I concluded that life was too short to be unhappy. It was time for me to move on.

CHAPTER NINE: MOVING ON

"You can spend minutes, hours, days, weeks, or even months over-analyzing a situation; trying to put the pieces together, justifying what could've, would've happened… or you can just leave the pieces on the ground and move on." - Tupac Shakur

It's very hard to explain, everything was shattered, and I was left in ruins.

Every time I tried to forget Beeba, something out of nowhere knocks me on the head and everything came back to me. I suffered emotionally, and even psychologically. Heck! My grades suffered.

Moving on is tricky; you try to get a new hobby, do things that you love, meet new people. Slowly, your mind starts to clear up... Well, until you see or hear about that one person you have been trying so hard to move on from, then everything turns new, the pain and anguish – every tiny bit of it.

A few months after Beeba and I parted ways, I met a girl that I knew was her cousin. We started to hit off very quickly, we became very close in a nick of time.

We had conversations about our past relationships, and how her ex-boyfriend cheated on her with Beeba.

Things between us started to get serious. She was someone I talked to all the time.

Talking to her came with a feeling of guilt, something about it felt off, it felt like I was using her to get away from a feeling I was traumatized by.

I decided to talk to Khairiyyah, since after all, she knew all that happened.

Khairiyyah thought it was a bad idea to get into something serious or even continue talking with her.

Before I could even end it, everything began to fade, everything between us died a natural death.

Moving on is not just forgetting someone, it's learning to live without them. Most of the time, it's not the person we miss, it's the routine that we were so used to.

I was so used to talking with Beeba all the time, I didn't even know what to do with my time anymore. It's funny how loving someone could make you lose yourself.

My heart was broken, but my vision was corrected.

I could see clearly how the world works. Nobody is ever going to love you the way you deserve, you got to love yourself before anyone else does. And no matter how close you are to someone or how long you have known each other, they'll still cancel on you the moment something better in their eyes comes along.

It's everyone for himself. Survival of the fittest.

CHAPTER TEN: THE BEGINNING OF THE END

Time flies even when you are not having fun.

The school had open and we were already in our fourth year. It seemed like it was just yesterday when I walked through the gates of the university with my hair cut low and my cheeks smooth as a baby's forehead.

I walked on the pavement by the side of the road passing by the school football field that was wire fenced.

It was during the early hours of the day when I was about to start my first-year registration.

There was a clear sky, the sun was blazing with most of its Rays blocked by the branches and leaves of the tall trees planted all over the school which formed light beams all on the streets.

The buildings were flat and looked a bit ancient – not the image of a university I had in mind.

Wearing my favorite faded blue jeans with a white Ralph Lauren shirt, I had my backpack filled with rather unnecessary stuff, documents, and whatnot.

I walked swiftly pass a lot of people that looked at me with piety in their eyes, and some that were mostly freshmen like myself gave me welcoming smiles.

In my fourth year already, I couldn't believe it was me that had just a year to graduate, I used to see the senior students that were in their fourth and fifth year like Rock stars or Superheroes of some sort. It was my time, and it just didn't feel the way I imagined.

It was the semester before our industrial training, there was still a little seriousness left in us. Classes started early and we attended just as early as they started.

There were a lot of new faces, that year, the school took in new students in huge numbers.

Rio and I went to attend our second class of the semester at the phase one building of the faculty of environmental technology.

It was a single-story building with a flat roof that was painted with orange on the edges and cream on the rest of the building.

There was a Blue Toyota sedan parked in the entrance porch that was crowded with many people all waiting for a thing or two.

The environmental garden with several white-painted gazebos where Rio and I normally sit and wait for lectures to begin was located just opposite the Phase one building.

The garden was bounded by Curbstones that were painted in black and white. And within this garden, many trees provided a lot of shade.

Just when we were about to find a place to sit, I decided that I need to get a notebook.

We took off from the garden and down to a Shop just after the school library where they sold books and other writing materials.

On our way down to the Shop, just after the postgraduate mosque opposite an engineering building, some girls were walking towards us, and apparently to the garden we just left. These girls were three in number, all covered up in long Hijabs.

My eyes caught the lady in ash, and the other girls were just blank in my eyes. I stared into her eyes for split seconds and we passed them by.

Just after purchasing the notebook, I received a phone call from our class representative that the lecturer was already at the parking lot just opposite the phase one building before the environmental garden.

Rio and I walked hurriedly to meet with our class representative.

We met Faiz standing by the trunk of an old ash Honda Accord by the car parking lot, he was with a woman who was supposed to be the one that would lecture us on contract law.

We met the two of them and said our greetings, the woman was dark and not very tall.

From afar, I was panicking hoping she wouldn't be as rude or as hard as she looked.

After exchanging a few words, I realized that she was actually nice and jovial, and very good at what she does, at that instant I knew we were on for a ride.

Standing by the parking lot, while Rio and Faiz were conversing with our lecturer trying to come up with a lecture time, I caught the eyes I lost myself in earlier.

It was the girl from the engineering complex, she was standing by a gazebo in the environmental garden while her friends were seated on the park benches.

♫ I'm staring at you from afar, I'm wondering about you Like, where you from and who you are? 'Cause you a star—no, not the type that snorts the white lines. I mean the type to light the night time♫

Her eyes were very white and sharp, courtesy of the outline made by her long dark eyelashes. If it was during night time, her eyes would shine brighter than a thousand stars.

She wore a long hijab that covered most of her body with only her face and feet to spare.

Her black and ash flip flops blended perfectly with her ash hijab, and somehow made her slim well-trimmed toenails brighter.

Our eyes locked and my soul was lost to a ravishing smile, I couldn't stop looking into her eyes as she was looking right back into mine.

I have always found eye contact awkward and weird, I usually looked away the moment I got myself in the act. But with this girl everything felt different, I got love strokes rather than awkward feelings. I couldn't look away.

I was completely lost. I just knew there was something about her and I was up to the task of finding out.

Our lecturer and class representative decided we should hold an introductory class that morning. And off we went into the phase one building and to a lecture room set aside for our department.

Over the lecture, all I could think of was this girl that gave me butterflies in the early hours of the day. It was my first time seeing her in school or anywhere. She must be a freshman. And considering where I saw her, she must be in our faculty.

All the time I had spent in the university, I had never met a girl I was so much into and was willing to approach and not just admire from afar than this girl.

I started to ask questions about her. Who she was, where she was from, and the department she was in.

Luckily, Faiz already knew who she was. She was the only girl admitted to our department that year.

"You better keep off. This one is mine." Jokingly, Faiz said.

Sometimes, when I want something and happen to be all in for it, luck finds me.

Rio was then the President of the students of our department, he had everyone's listening ears and was highly respected, especially amongst the new intakes.

He promised to get me her name and her number since he knew she was in our department. I thought he was just pulling my leg.

Sometime after, on a Thursday evening, he came to me with a name and a phone number, it was at that moment I realized that the court had been set and the ball was already rolling.

Amila, such a beautiful name I thought.

My experience of calling a stranger on the phone was a shady one, there was no way I could do that again. And since this girl was in my school, I thought it was better to get her contact myself.

I refused to accept the contact, and I informed Rio of my intentions.

The next day which was Friday and there was only one lecture to attend that morning.

I wore a traditional maroon kaftan with a matching cap and a black sandal looking all responsible.

Getting to the class, we found out there was already a lecture going on where we were supposed to have ours. Amila was there in the class, it was their lecture going on.

Rio told me he would pull an act just after the class, all I needed to do was follow his lead. He handed me a pen and a piece of paper.

He left me speculating, I was both frightened and thrilled at the same time. I didn't know what it was he was planning but deep down I was praying and hoping for the successful execution of his plan.

We stood by the door and held our fire until their lecturer who was then our Head of Department walked out.

Immediately he walked out of the class, Rio charged into the room, and I, holding a pen and a piece of paper followed him in like a tail.

Amila was sedentary just by the door. She was wearing a blue with a touch of red traditional top and skirt, and a short fine red veil tied on her head and around her neck that spread over her shoulders.

Her brown skin shone like gold. Her eyes seem brighter and her eyelashes darker. Her skin was smooth and shiny like a polish finish.

Rio gave the class a hand gesture asking everyone to sit down. He presented himself as the President he was, and me, as his chief of staff.

He told them he was going to organize tutorial classes for them, and they should say out the courses they were finding tough while I pen them down.

I chuckled and watched towards her direction. She was looking at me, and I caught her in the act.

The other students were all stating out course codes but all my devotion was on the price before of me.

She spoke out a course code, and I looked at her and grinned.

After coming up with a list, Rio and I took our leave.

We met a number of our friends at the environmental garden, and just like that, the meeting turned to a photoshoot.

After everything, I still didn't get Amila's contact. But Rio was going to hold freshmen welcoming and orientation lunch in a week. I thought that would be my last Chance.

Time flew quickly like it always does, it was already the day of the orientation.

I was with Usman and Auwal that faithful Saturday afternoon, Rio kept on calling me on the phone. The Lunch was about to start, and the speech he would give out was with me.

Auwal who was also our classmate and my friend rushed me to where the event was taking place just when the president was about to deliver his speech. Right on time.

The room where the event was taking place was a classroom that was decorated accordingly for the event.

The high table was faced by the rows of seats occupied by the freshmen and the podium where the president would be delivering his speech from was just adjacent to the high table.

I found myself a seat at the back with just a row behind and made myself at home.

The event was going on while I was texting on my phone when suddenly I felt a presence behind me, I turned around and I saw Amila. She was alone, dressed in a black Abaya. *This is my chance, I can't mess this up.*

I stood there mute for a while thinking of what to say and what not to. I couldn't Garner enough Courage, but I knew that was the perfect opportunity.

"Amila, right?"

"Yes. Good afternoon" she responded.

"How are you?" I asked, "Have you guys started the tutorial yet?"

I was trying very hard not to freeze and kill the conversation in the process. I was about to ask as many questions as possible, I was about to ask for her contact – like a man.

"We are still waiting," she responded.

"I'll talk to the president. And while I am at it, I'll get your contact too" I said.

Just as our conversation was about to end, a guy came in to join her. And a little while after, they left.

After going back to our room at the end of the day, I told Rio everything that transpired, and we laughed about it. At that instant, he gave me her number and I called.

Before I told her who I was, she was answering me rudely. But that quickly changed.

We started to hit off quickly. We were always texting, always talking on the phone, and in no time we became very close.

We met in school often, we took long walks together which made everyone in school believed we were together.

The semester was about to end, and we were going for Industrial training which meant I wouldn't be in school with them the next semester.

I tried very hard to spend a lot of time with her. And in the process, I fell in love with her before I could even realize it.

All my years at the university, I had never fallen in love, I had always thought I'd graduate without having dated any girl. But Amila, in just a matter of months changed my perspective on everything.

After Beeba, I was afraid of falling in love again, I was afraid of being broken again, but not anymore. I was willing to risk it all with Amila.

CHAPTER ELEVEN: A BEAUTIFUL DISASTER

"You like someone who can't like you back because unrequited love can be survived in a way that once-requited love cannot." John Green

You'd be Keen and anxious about having your proposal accepted thinking after that everything would magically turn glittery.

You'd have dreams, ideas, and thoughts on how to make everything worthwhile. What we think often indeed makes our reality, but it's also true that a reality that concerns two people has to be made by these people.

Amila agreed to us dating. All I have ever wanted, all my thoughts had been revolving around for months.

"We can date"

The words kept on going back and forth on my mind. I was highly elated, I didn't even know what to make of it, my aptitude to speak, or even type gone all in a matter of seconds. For some time, it was all I wanted to hear. She was all I wanted.

She was officially my girlfriend, and I thought all the feelings of great mental distress and discomfort would go away. I was played to my surprise.

Everything went on the way they were, I was still being ignored. My calls were still not answered, and when they got answered she spoke to me in a manner that always sent a subconscious message that I was just not important to her.

It's possible to be together with someone and yet be lonely. I was lonely, sick, and depressed. I was so ashamed of my story that I couldn't tell it to anyone, it was emotional cancer that was eating me up slowly.

It was towards the end of my Industrial Training. All I looked forth to was waking up very early in the morning to go to work and come back home and sleep early at night just to repeat the whole process the next day.

I was stuck in a seemingly endless loop. I was alive but I wasn't truly living.

I started listening to spoken word poetry and writing pieces of poetry for the first time in my life that I'd give Usman to read every time He came to visit me during the weekends. I had no one I wanted to tell, but I always had my Note to run back to.

I didn't want in anymore, but I was anchored down by the love I had for her.

It didn't feel like moving on anymore. It felt like I moved from the frying pan to the fire flames.

With the truthiness of the love I felt towards her, I knew I had to talk to her and make things right, I knew I couldn't continue with the way we were moving. I thought it was best to talk – to communicate.

I just came back from work, sitting in my room that was all in the darkness just how I liked it. Everything was calm and silent. I could hear the whistling sound of the crickets, I could hear my thoughts.

With nothing to do but sleep, I decided to talk to Amila about our relationship and how we needed to work on it.

"Ever since you agreed to us, nothing has changed. I feel like I am the only one in this relationship" I said

"It's not like that" after a very long while, she replied.

"If there is anything wrong, don't you think we should sit down and talk it out?" I asked.

"The truth is, I only said yes because I didn't want to hurt your feelings" she uttered.

I was confused, I didn't know what to say anymore.

"I am sorry, but we can still be friends." She added.

That was it for me. *I am never going to try it again, I am done.*

I told her it was okay and that was it. I decided to give her a lot of space, I decided I want to forget her completely. So I took the course.

I didn't talk to Amila for about a month, it wasn't easy but it was what I needed to do.

Love isn't always shiny, sometimes it's just blunt like the edges of an overused ax. I loved and lost, and that was okay.

They say that winners never quit, that patience and time changes everything. I tried very hard not to quit, but I was always losing. I tried time and patience, but my mental health hung in the balance.

I quit! If that was the cost of loving someone truly, then I didn't want to anymore. But that wasn't really up to me.

It's true that when you loved someone truly, there is no unloving them. You'd still care, and you'd still want to hear from them sometimes.

To stop loving someone you truly loved is like an impossibility. But for me, impossible was nothing.

I decided to look for ways one could stop loving someone. My internet searches were all on love and how to become heartless, and my conversations were all about love. I was hopeless and desperate. At that moment all I wanted to be was a stoic.

After a long failed quest of erasing an impossibility, I spoke with Ibrahim, a good friend of mine that I met in the university. He was the ladies guy who once tried love and failed.

I asked for his insight, he was hesitant for a moment, then he sent me a screenshot of a google search about love.

You can't stop loving someone that you once upon a time loved truly, the only thing you can do is find someone that you love more, and everything fades in time.

At that moment, I realized that it was an impossibility that meant something. And there was no way around the idea.

Maybe I loved a little too much. People often said I Love too deeply, I thought that was a good thing but then I found myself questioning my ideal. All I ever got from love was a deteriorating self-esteem.

The first few days of letting go weren't entirely easy. To sleep at night became a hard endeavor. I'd stay up all night thinking of what could have been, or where I went wrong.

But just like it does to everything, Time made my worries fade. I slept on time, I became more confident, and I could feel my self-esteem revamping. I began to glow like I was supposed to.

CHAPTER TWELVE: THE BUMPY RIDE

On a Saturday, the morning came and blessed us with a burst of blissful sunshine after a run of the foggy atmosphere.

I was done with my industrial training, and all that I was looking forth to was my trip back home.

I drove into the gates of the legislative quarters. There were trees planted at both sides of the street and everywhere was covered in shades. Local traders and everyone was going about his normal business like it was not even a Saturday.

I picked up my phone and dialed up Usman to inform him I was by the gate of their house, even before I got there. On my arrival, I met him waiting for me by the gate.

We got in and I helped him pack his luggage. While we were at it, my phone started to ring, I couldn't believe my eyes. It was Amila.

I was in shock. I could feel the rate of my heartbeat harshly increasing. I kept staring at my phone, wondering if it was true or it was just a figment of my imaginations.

It appeared like I lost the aptitude to move, I froze and stared at the phone until it rang no more. *Why is she calling me?*

I was trying to move on and forget her, and she was trying to keep me hostage. I didn't want to talk to her anymore, I didn't want her anymore, but I still loved her.

I told Usman that she just called me and that I wasn't planning on calling back. He insisted I must. I agreed to call her back, but not right away.

On the way home, we stopped at Ummi's place to tell her of our plan to leave for Bauchi the next day. We said our goodbyes and left for home later that evening while it was raining heavily.

We got in and met Aunty Nafy in the sitting room who was in the company of two of her beautiful kids, Musnaf and Musaddiq. We had a very long chat. She was trying to persuade us not to leave the next day, but there was no way we were going to change our minds.

We were there for six months, and it felt like it wasn't more than six days.

Before the night ran out, I called Amila back. And we had a very short conversation that she only wanted to say hi.

I went to sleep, and it was morning again. I checked on the car, everyone took his shower, and we were ready to hit the road.

Aunty Nafy offered us breakfast, and because we didn't normally eat before embarking on a journey, we declined.

Aunty Nafy in her long brown hijab and Musaddiq came out and stood by the door to say goodbye. She didn't want us to leave, her face was paled and her eyes were brimmed up with tears, even though she was strong enough not to let them flow, her voice let her down.

I asked where Musnaf was, and apparently, she was inside crying, she couldn't come out to say goodbye.

I was very emotional, if I had stayed there for a few more minutes, I would have disappeared into a puddle of tears.

We embarked on the journey very early in the morning, just before getting out of Abuja, we stopped by a shop to buy water and yogurt.

The journey started nicely, we were moving at a constant speed of 120km/h. And according to our calculation, we would be in Bauchi by 1 pm.

The road was peaceful as we made progress. The weather was a foggy one, there was no sunshine, which made the environment cooler.

We had already made significant progress, we were almost halfway there when the car started to misbehave. The temperature was rising rapidly. I didn't know what to make of it, neither did Usman.

We decided to stop at a filling station to add up water to the radiator, and we did even before the car cooled down not knowing we were creating an even bigger problem.

After filling up the radiator, we proceeded with the journey. We stopped by some hawkers and bought a few bunches of banana.

After a while, the car started to overheat again. But we didn't stop anywhere, and at short intervals, we would discontinue and add up water. The farther we went, the lower the interval.

It was already 4 pm, and we were just a few kilometers away from Bauchi when we stopped at a mosque in a filling station to pray. After we have already prayed, I far-sighted a mechanic workshop just across the road and we decided to check them out.

The workshop was an open space just by the road. We went there and told them what the car had been doing, and they immediately figured out what the problem was and that there was no way they could work on it while the engine was still hot.

We waited for the engine to cool down. It was 5:30 pm already. We were famished and dog-tired. There was no food, and it skipped our minds to ask where we could get any in the little village.

We started eating the bananas like we were some sort of monkeys until we exhausted 3 bunches. We were still starving, well at least I was.

The mechanics worked on the engine until it was dark, and that there was something in there that got burnt and must be replaced.

Well, that was okay. Except the gasket replacement must be bought at a nearby city. We had to wait until the next morning.

I gave my dad a call and he advised us to find a motel and spend the night there. But in Magama village, there was no Bank or even an ATM, there was no way we could find a Motel.

Before we could even ponder over it, the mechanic that looked like he was in his early twenties, without the knowledge of who we were or where we came from offered us his room to spend the night. With little or no option, we accepted the offer.

At that moment, all our mobile phones were dead on battery and there was no electricity then.

We followed him to a room and he left us there. The room was small and very hot, with no window, and I was scared I could get sick. I knew it was going to be a very long night.

I had a story I couldn't wait to tell but there was no one to tell it to. There was no Amila. Every time I thought of her I became feeble and in no time I got covered up by a gloomy feeling.

I couldn't wait to get home. I hated the road not only because of the misfortune but also because I missed home.

The next morning I woke up fully energetic, thinking the mechanic would run to the nearby city and get the gaskets very early. I was convinced we'd leave before the afternoon. But unfortunately, the mechanic couldn't fix the car on time. We didn't leave for Bauchi until it was 7 pm with the car that was partially fixed.

CHAPTER THIRTEEN: LIFE HAPPENS

"It's just life, it'll be over before you know it." - Will Newman (Five feet apart).

We were back in school, done with our industrial training, and there were only two semesters left for us to graduate. I couldn't wait. Mostly because of Amila.

The school didn't interest me anymore. I just wanted to be done and get myself out of that place. I hoped time would magically fly.

I normally stayed around the school in a rented apartment with Mahmoud. But that semester I wasn't really into it, I was on and off. I decided on going to school from home just so that I could avoid Amila as much as possible.

It was a Friday morning at the beginning of the semester, I drove to the school with Al-Musty. I dropped him at one of the hostels where he would meet Ishaq, and I drove off to our departmental building.

Getting to our department, I found out that there was nothing to do that morning, I was free for the day.

I decided to go and meet Al-Musty and Ishaq, and maybe while away sometime before it was time for prayer.

I met them at the hostel, they were just chatting and had no apparent thing to do.

Ishaq suggested that we drive to their rendezvous. It was a place right behind their hostel and next to a restaurant. Many trees gave out a lot of shade that provided some coolness even when the weather was hot.

Getting to the point, we met a group of girls and some boys. A photo-shoot was at play. One of the boys that were with a camera was taking their pictures, and one of the girls whose pictures were taken was Amila.

A sense of nervousness hit me. My hands started to shake, and my voice started to tremble. I wished I had not followed the bandwagon.

She wore a long ash Abaya with a black scarf. She looked thinner and different, and she was wearing a lot of makeup which turned her complexion to a darker one. I wanted to say something but I kept it to myself.

After saying my greetings to the group, I stood there awkwardly and kept my mouth shut. I was in the 'smile and wave' mood until it was time for us to leave and we said our goodbyes.

"I don't know who told girls they look beautiful with make-up" sarcastically, Ishaq uttered. *And I thought I was the only one.*

The feeling came back to me again, which I barely got through. I was feeling blue, I craved for her attention, and I craved for her soothing voice. But I knew the best for me was to just stay away, and think of her as nothing more than just a friend to the highest extent.

After a few hours of sleep, I managed to shake off the feeling of blue that ate through me all through the day. That was the reason why I was trying to avoid her. It was like a course, she was a Demon I couldn't seem to shake off.

Some weeks after, I was in school to study for a test I was supposedly going to write that weekend. I came out of the library and I was walking to Ibrahim's room at a nearby hostel where I normally go to rest after every long day before going home.

I walked by the shops down the school library, looking downwards as if I was counting my steps, and gently swung back and forth the rolled lecture note on my right hand and just thinking about the things that I just studied.

As if it was whispered into my ears, suddenly, I raised my head and what I saw was a slim girl in a brown traditional Hausa attire. She was walking in my direction.

The heart in my chest started to pound heavily, I could feel an excessive heat coming from within me. The oxygen I was breathing seemed to be exhausted. I thought I was going to have a heart attack.

We walked closer to each other covering the gap between us. To my surprise, it wasn't Amila.

Her silhouette, the way she wiggled her slender body side to side like a pendulum as she walked, how slowly she walked, her complexion, and the way she kept looking towards my direction made me believe it was Amila. I was relieved.

I walked my way passed this girl to Ibrahim's room and said a little prayer in my mind. *I pray I never see Amila again.*

I met Ibrahim watching on his computer as he always does. Bukar, Nu'man, and Nazif were all gathered around trying to solve a Math problem. And Abdulhakim was charging his phone by the wall socket that was under the large window, this was while he was seated on the floor with his back against the wall, and his legs crossed as if he was meditating.

I told Ibrahim what happened and we both laughed about it, even when I didn't find it funny.

After a while, KB came in and we started to talk about poetry and a book he was working on.

Ibrahim, Bukar, and Nazif stayed in the same room that whole session. The room was like a rendezvous for us, every day we all met there for no apparent reason. Sometimes, we played video games, watched movies, and sometimes we discussed books and theories.

Ibrahim was done with his movie, a few of our friends came in and were heading out to the library, and Ibrahim and I decided to join the bandwagon.

On our way back from the library, at the exact spot I met the girl that looked just like Amila, I far-sighted her.

She was the one this time around. She was standing in our path with some girls and a boy that was speaking very loudly, a boy I happened to know. None of them were looking towards our direction.

I decided to look the other way and act as if I had not seen them, and I begged Ibrahim to do the same. We walked slowly passed them hoping none of them would notice. Suddenly, a feeling of Déjà vu stroke.

Just after we have passed them by, Ibrahim tapped me at the back. And when I turned to look at him, he pointed towards their direction. They saw us passing and Amila asked the boy they were with to call our attention.

I stopped, and she came over to where I stood. We said our greetings. But there was nothing more to say to her.

"There is something we need to do right now. So I guess I'll see you around." I said.

"I'll call you," she said before we could turn around and move our way.

I couldn't fathom what was going on. She was trying to act as if everything was fine between us when truly nothing was. But we were friends, and I planned to stick to that. After all, she was so much a better friend to me than she was a girlfriend.

After I have gone back home, she called me and we spoke for a little while.

A friend of mine had already told me about the lad she was dating when she agreed to us. How he wasn't as into her as she was into him. He broke up with her and broke her heart in the process.

I quickly forgot about myself and I was already feeling sorry for her. I thought maybe she was hurt very badly that was why she hurt me the way she did. I knew that wasn't a justification, but I justified her actions because I loved her.

I met her a few times afterward. I was trying to be a good friend to her, I felt sorry for her.

Sometime after, we decided to meet in front of their hostel before I leave for home.

I waited for her in front of their hostel for a few minutes, and she showed up in a brown traditional gown. It was dark, but she was still glowing.

We talked for a while, and while we were at it, I decided to ask her about her boyfriend. She broke into tears, and it broke my heart. I wanted to be there for her, and I told her. She was still crying her eyes out, and for some reason, she couldn't tell me why and claimed the tears were just as a result of an allergic reaction.

******

Fast-forward to the day I completed my first-semester examination.

Amila and I decided to meet up that nightfall before my trip to Gombe the next day, but regrettably, Magjee who was then our Student Union Government president called me that he was on our other campus that was remotely located as his car had broken down. I had to leave earlier than anticipated.

I went back home that night and it started to rain. I sat by the sockets and began to chat on my phone while it charged.

A message from Amila came in, that we needed to talk. Somehow, I knew what the tête-à-tête would be about – our relationship.

She couldn't text me what she wanted to express to me, that she would call me instead. But I wasn't prepared to catch anything right then, I knew what transpired the last time and how I was touched by it. I was wary of its reoccurrence.

"It's raining here, and I won't be able to hear you clearly on the phone. But I'll call you later when it's not raining." I said to her.

It was a lie I told her to buy myself some time to think about getting in a relationship, even before she uttered her intents.

I called Mahmoud, then I called Usman. I expressed to them what I was facing, and they both told me the same thing. That I should settle on a relationship with her and find my way if she ever repeated what she did, or if I ever felt uninvited.

I called her. It was just as I projected. She wanted us to try again. I was okay with that, but then I recapped to her what came about the first time, and told her I could not handle that again.

We got into a relationship again. This time around, everything appeared differently. It was as if she was a different person. She didn't disregard my messages, and she returned my calls as soon as it was possible for her.

As time went by, the energy she was putting in the relationship started to decline. It was just like history repeating itself all over again. But I have already made a promise to myself never to put in more energy than I get in return again.

She left my messages unread and I returned the favor by not sending them anymore. Though I kept on calling her, she never called or returned my calls when they were missed.

I thought maybe she didn't check up on me because I was always checking up on her. I decided to give her a little space and see if at all she'd notice my absence.

A week and some days went by and I didn't hear from her. I decided to talk to her.

I talked to her about our relationship, how she didn't check up on me, and how we could only make our relationship work through effective communication.

"Just because we are in a relationship doesn't necessarily mean we should be communicating all the time," she said and cut me off on my track.

After everything, for me, that was the last straw. I was the only one trying, and at that moment I knew I was the only one in the relationship. It was over.

I understood that no matter how much you love someone, sometimes, the best thing you can do is to let them go.

You cannot force anyone to love you. Love doesn't work that way. But it's just like Umaima said: "if you don't like someone tell them so that they can move on"

There is no point in staying in a relationship you aren't interested in just because you don't want to hurt the other party involved. To hurt them by telling them the truth is always better than to hurt them by lying to them.

I might have been hurt by those whom I cared for, I might have felt betrayed, but none of it would matter in years to come. Heck! I might not even remember.

To forgive is to live in peace with oneself. We all make mistakes, and that's what makes us human.

Many have lived before us and many would probably live after us. Many that came before us are nothing now but lost memories.

This life as we see it may seem like much. It passes by slowly yet it flies. You're playing on your grandparent's lap now, and in no time your grandchild is playing on yours.

There is no reason to be stressed or unhappy over things that one cannot change, things that are just as temporary as life itself.

When life happens, there is nothing we can do about it. However, to understand and live by that is a humongous blessing.

ACKNOWLEDGEMENTS

May the peace of Allah and his endless blessings be upon the seal of the prophet, Muhammad (peace be upon him), his household, and those that follow his righteousness till the day of reckoning (Amen).

I want to thank the almighty Allah for making it possible for me to write even when I thought I couldn't, for giving me the wisdom and the courage to.

My appreciation goes to my family, most especially my parents for the moral upbringing, guidance, and endless support. May Allah reward you abundantly.

I want to express my profound gratitude and appreciation to my friends; Yusuf Aminu, Usman Ismail, Mahmoud Abdulsalam Yidi, Abubakar Ahmed Sani, Muhammad Auwal Sani, Muhammad Tukur Umar, Muhammad Aminu Umar, Abdulhakim Auwal, Ahmad Shazali Suleiman, Isah Umar Abdulqadir and Sadiq Sani Yaro, Thank you for being there for me when I needed you guys the most. The memories we shared will forever be cherished.

To Suleiman Jafar, kabiru Abdullahi and Hadiyya Tilde, I appreciate your intellects and the endless support I got from you guys from the onset.

To Ibrahim Abdullahi and Bukar Kachalla, thank you for all the advice.

My Jaruma, Aisha Ishaq Salihu. There aren't enough words to describe how much appreciative of you I am. You are a great friend and an amazing human being. Thank you for simply being you

To my Rock Star, Firdausi Umar Ajingi. Even if I find myself in a sea of people, I'd still search for you. You are my rock and the star in my sky.

There is no way I will forget Maryam Saidu Alkali. You were there for me when I had no one to turn back to, you showed me love and made me realize that even a shattered glass glitter when you let in a little light, and for that I am forever grateful. Thank you.

Lastly, I will like to thank Her Excellency the first lady of Kaduna state, Hajiya Isma El-Rufai whom I have learnt a lot from through the twitter hashtag she leads, #KadunaLanguageClasss. You are a true inspiration. Thank you.

ABOUT THE AUTHOR

Photo by Saidu Adamu Degri

MARZUQ UMAR BASHIR was born in Bauchi, raised in Kaduna, and lives in Gombe State, Nigeria. He is an occasional Poet whose achievement is publishing his Poems on social media, and being shortlisted for Earnest Writers' Poetry Prize Awards 2020. He has a bachelor's degree in Building Technology from Abubakar Tafawa Balewa University, Bauchi. *Life happens...* is his first Novel. You can find him online on Twitter and Instagram @Mvrzuq.

CREDITS

Cover page - designed by Suleiman Kole

Song Lyrics - from the song Déjà vu by Jermaine Cole (J. Cole)